D'Leaux, Mississippi

Life From Moss to Tuckertown

Cecil George Brown

D'Leaux, Mississippi

Life From Moss to Tuckertown

A NOVEL IN STORIES BY

CECIL GEORGE BROWN

ISBN: 978-1-7369441-1-0 (paperback)
ISBN: 978-1-7369441-0-3 (ebook)

Cover photo courtesy of Morris Brown

Book cover and interior design by TeaBerry Creative

For Nancy Pollina Ford

D'Leaux, Mississippi began as a series of emails I exchanged with my friend and editor Nancy Pollina Ford. I shared stories of Cecil McRae Britton as Nancy shared exploits of her dear sister Zenith. Poor Zenith, she could not be saved from herself. Cecil McRae soon controlled the narrative and D'Leaux came to life. This book would not exist without Nancy Ford and her kind but firm insistence that I step aside. Cecil McRae must speak for herself.

Thank you, Nancy.

Contents

The Rabbit Trap 1

The Bobwhites 7

The *Ami Du Coeur* 13

The Curse 19

The Silver Dollars 23

The Christmas Gift 29

The Honeymoon 37

Washington D.C. 43

The Piano Recital 51

The Underwear 55

The Cats 65

The Kidnapping 73

The Doughnuts 79

The Play 87

The Top Hat Club 93

The Chicken Salad 99

The Grief Process 105

Orange Poppies 111

The Feed Store 113

The Beauty Pageant 117

Miss Toufet.. 123

The Christmas Star... 131

The Peanuts.. 139

The Grave 145

The Homecoming... 149

Discussion Guide for D'Leaux, Mississippi............................ 155

Acknowledgements 163

About the Author 165

D'Leaux, Mississippi

Life From Moss to Tuckertown

The Rabbit Trap

Alice Faye Turner was the worst girl in D'Leaux Elementary. She said bad words in front of the teachers, threatened to kill the principal's pigs, and kicked, punched, or bit anybody stupid enough to walk past her desk. I couldn't believe it when Alice Faye took over my yard, but she did. It happened the year Uncle Dewey left his job to finish school, and he and Aunt Ruby moved home with us.

Uncle Dewey hired Clifton Turner to chip and dip pines. Clifton Turner was Alice Faye's daddy. People don't collect pine rosin these days. But working the Piney Woods used to be big business. About the end of September, crews of men would go through the woods chipping sections of bark from the trees and hammering a metal trough underneath the chip. Rosin would ooze out of the tree into the trough. It's yellow and gummy. In really cold weather, the sap looks like sugar candy all crusty and white on the top, but don't eat it. Pine rosin is really bitter and will stick to your teeth forever. Later, the men would dip the rosin from the troughs into barrels for processing. That's what Uncle Dewey hired Clifton Turner to do: chip the pines then dip the rosin.

Money from our trees plus the GI Bill got Uncle Dewey through his engineering degree. My brother Grady saw his future that year, and I practiced being kind.

Clifton Turner and Alice Faye had an old travel trailer parked behind the Tiara Ballroom and Movie Theatre on Short Street. When Mr. Maddox tore the building down, the trailer had to go. That's how Clifton and Alice Faye came to live at our pump house. Mama said they could hook up to electricity and water right at the pump and were welcomed to stay as long as Clifton worked for Uncle Dewey.

Alice Faye's mother, Juanita, was serving time at Parchman. Everybody knew that. Years later, I learned Juanita Turner wrote bad checks. That's what got her in prison; but in third grade, I knew—everybody knew—Alice Faye's mama was a criminal.

Miss Hightower, the third grade teacher, couldn't handle Alice Faye. After that year, Miss Hightower stopped school teaching and went to work at the welfare office. She never said so but Miss Hightower left D'Leaux Elementary School because of Alice Faye Turner. Alice Faye never stood in line. And it didn't matter how long she took at the water fountain after recess. She didn't even get paddled the time she snatched Priscilla Jane Jenkins' Cinderella lunch box and threw it across the cafeteria. All Miss Hightower said was, "Sit by yourself, Alice, until you're sure you're sorry."

"What good's that going to do, Mama," I complained. "Alice Faye is never going to be sorry, and she wants to sit by herself anyway."

"Would you like to sit with Aunt Ruby a while, Little Bit? She might enjoy some company about now."

Having a baby isn't as easy as it looks. Aunt Ruby's heart wasn't right. She fainted. All the time she was waiting for Robert Earl, she had to rest. Mama moved a bed into the living room so she could hear the radio and we took turns carrying her things to and from the kitchen.

It was the most fun ever helping Aunt Ruby. We would pretend the bed was magic and I was a princess. Aunt Ruby was the evil magician. She would cast the magic spell, and I had to be whatever she said. Sometimes I had to be a frog and hop around until she tapped me on the head. Or maybe she would say, "Butterfly." Then I had to roll up into my cocoon and lie perfectly still until she named all the stars in the eastern sky. The best game was Wishes and Horses. In that game, we had to wish all about a place to go and name the horse to take us there. My favorite place was the Arizona Badlands and my horse was Fire Dancer. Rodeos and Indian fights and prospecting for gold were always in my story and bank robbers with secret hangouts in the mountains.

Uncle Dewey spent the week in Starkville but came home about every weekend. He would haul the barrels of pine rosin to the distillery in Clear Creek. The place closed years ago. But at one time, you could taste turpentine in the air for miles around especially in winter. Clear Creek was a good forty miles below Windham so going and coming was a long day. Grady went almost every time. I remember going only once. The huge rusty distillery shambled down a hill toward the river, and all around the building was steamy and hot. The men running up and down didn't wear shirts but tied rags over their faces like bandits. Nothing about it looked fun.

Trouble with Alice Faye began the minute their dilapidated tin box of a trailer got settled in my yard. She started collecting everything she could find then stacking it behind the pump house. And Mama started harping on me to be kind. My bicycle, my wagon, my jump rope. Everything. Even my baby buggy. If I so much as left an empty Cracker Jack box outside, Alice Faye stole it. Then she'd sit in the trailer door with a big pile of dirt clods and a slingshot.

"No one is stealing, Little Bit," Mama insisted. "Have you asked Mr. Turner about your things?"

Mama was no smarter than Miss Hightower. If Clifton Turner with his jailbird wife was "Mr. Turner," then nothing was happening to Alice Faye.

"What you might do, Little Bit," Mama said, "is practice being kind."

"What about Alice Faye," I complained. "Can't she be kind? That's my baby buggy. I'm saving it. Aunt Ruby said it's big enough to hold a real baby. I'm not giving my baby buggy that my baby cousin is going to ride in to Alice Faye Turner."

I wasn't giving Alice Faye anything.

I took all my dolls to the back porch and played hospital. I sat on the back steps and put puzzles together and played dominos by myself and won every game. One day I made the porch into a fort with bed sheets for walls and a real flag. I played Indians and cavalry with Grady's cap guns and pretended to hold myself hostage until Buffalo Bill rescued me and we got married.

Then the worst thing happened. Our mama kitty Bluebell got caught in a rabbit trap. Her front leg was all flat and bloody. She

4

didn't move or even blink when Grady laid her down on a pallet in his room.

I knew all about traps. Uncle Otis made money as a boy trapping all sorts of things then selling the hides. Once he caught a red fox with a bushy black tail just like in the "Gingerbread Man." Every time he told about the fox, he chased me around and around the house until my sides hurt from squealing. Three or four rusty old traps still hung in the barn.

"Nobody has a right to trap our rabbits on our land, Mama. Nobody. Now Bluebell's dead and it's your fault."

Bluebell wasn't dead. She lived. But she would have died had Grady not known what to do. He put her leg in a splint and fed her milk and water from an eyedropper. He gave her little sips every two hours for three whole days.

My performance on the porch went from being rescued by Buffalo Bill to praying for Bluebell's recovery. Sometimes I prayed so loud my voice got hoarse and I had to rest.

I sounded just like Brother Orion Marshall. Brother Marshall came to D'Leaux in the summer and held tent revivals by the courthouse. Everybody went, and a lot of people got saved. His Disciples for Jesus sold Coca Colas and parched peanuts before the service, and all the money went to help God's sinners gripped with fire and temptation.

Grady didn't like him, but I did.

"He's fake, Cecil McRae. He doesn't even have a real church, just an old army tent. And Sodom and Gomorrah burned up in the Bible. So how can we be living there? Brother Marshall says that to scare people."

I wanted to scare people too. I prayed for Bluebell and for God to punish all those people who trapped other people's cats when they ought to be grateful for a free place to live and an honest job paying twenty dollars a week.

Uncle Dewey took Bluebell back to State the next time he was home. She got well, but they cut off her leg. Dr. Ferguson from the vet school wrote Grady all about the operation and the splint. The splint was perfect, but the leg couldn't grow back. Bluebell would live and be just as happy with three legs as with four. Dr. Ferguson invited Grady to visit the animal hospital if we came for Uncle Dewey's graduation.

That May, Uncle Dewey graduated; Aunt Ruby had Robert Earl; and Grady got to see a baby horse being born. Mr. Turner found work at a meat processing plant so he and Alice Faye moved on to Moss.

And I got my stuff back. It lay in a heap behind the pump house: my bicycle, my wagon, my jump rope. Everything. Even my baby buggy filled with three dried rabbit hides neatly wrapped in brown paper and tied with twine.

The Bobwhites

The Willard treasure was a popular legend in Mounds County. Piles of gold were believed buried at Big Pine just waiting to be found. Lots of people wanted the treasure to be real. Some still do.

The Willard treasure has never been found, but it lost me a friend.

The idea of buried treasure got started soon after the war. Baxter Sandstrom Willard, my great grandpa, owned Big Pine Plantation. He farmed six thousand acres and worked at least three hundred slaves.

When the war ended, his slaves were gone and his crops burned. But nothing changed with Great Grandpa Willard. He was still "Master Willard" to anyone he met. When he walked into the courthouse, it was "Yes Sir, Master Willard" or "No Sir, Master Willard." He could still be Master Willard because he paid his taxes. During reconstruction, Black folks didn't have money and White folks who did wouldn't pay taxes to a Negro tax collector. Great Grandpa was the exception. Maybe he loved Big Pine so much he couldn't let it go, or maybe he loved being called "Master

Willard" by former slaves. Maybe neither. But from January 1866, until his death, Baxter Willard paid taxes on six thousand acres of abandoned wasteland. He paid his taxes completely, on time, and in gold. Twenty-dollar gold pieces to be exact.

The prevailing wisdom of Mounds County held he had left a vast treasure buried somewhere up at Big Pine. How could he not?

By the time he died in 1879 his own sons, my Grandma Rachel's brothers, were digging holes. They dug holes until they couldn't walk upright without a shovel, but they never found the treasure. No one has.

Hole diggers followed Grandma Rachel all her life even into the grave. She hadn't been in the ground a month before someone dug her up and ripped the lining out of her coffin.

Then her trunk went missing. One day, it was sitting at the foot of her bed; the next day, it was gone. "It's not fair for someone to tear up Grandma's coffin then steal her trunk," I said, "even if she is dead."

"It's the treasure," Grady said. "Great Grandpa's gold."

My brother Grady and me were down at the barn showing Mary Lou Morris the bobwhites. Grady was in his second year at State and I was helping him with a biology project. He had ordered thirty-six baby birds and was raising them in an old pheasant box. When they got bigger, he was turning them loose to live in the woods around the house.

Mary Lou had come to D'Leaux the summer Grandma Rachel died and was my new best friend. She loved being at our house and had practically moved in once we met. She had lived in Texas, Oklahoma, Louisiana and now Mississippi. Her daddy had a big job and made lots of money. He knew where highways were going to go and bought right of ways from people. That's why they lived in a trailer. One day soon, Mr. Morris was buying a big house in Vicksburg where he was from, and they were moving there. But for now, they lived in a house trailer parked down by Joiner's restaurant and drive-in.

Mrs. Morris drove a station wagon with air conditioning. And, she smoked. Chesterfields, like Mr. Williams, the shop teacher. I had never seen a woman smoke, and I had never ridden in an air-conditioned car. They were even getting an air conditioner for their trailer.

"We haven't gotten it yet," Mary Lou said, "but soon. One day I'll walk in from school and get so cold I'll need a jacket."

Mary Lou was really nice, but her brother Ronny was awful. He had yellow teeth and set fire to cats. While we were in Tuckertown for a football game, it was their homecoming, Ronny stole the band bus. The highway patrol caught him headed toward Meridian but couldn't take him to jail. He was too young. The principal Mr. McCann said he was a real juvenile delinquent and needed to be in military school or prison. He didn't care which.

"Grandma's coffin wasn't a treasure chest, Grady," I said showing Mary Lou how to quieten a baby bird by breathing on it, "and her trunk wasn't one either."

"I know that, Little Bit. But the robbers didn't."

"But the treasure's real, isn't it?" Mary Lou insisted. "Everybody says so."

"Whoever stole Grandma's trunk thought money was in it," Grady explained. "Or maybe they were looking for clues."

"Clues to the treasure," Mary Lou agreed. "They were looking for clues."

"There weren't any clues," I said. "Her trunk was packed full of old timey things like quilt squares pinned to newspaper and snuff cans full of buttons."

"But the treasure is hidden somewhere." Mary Lou insisted. "I bet we could find it if we knew where to look. My Uncle Raymond finds stuff all the time. He's good at it."

"Thinking about the treasure might be fun, Mary Lou, but the treasure isn't real," Grady said. "Looking for it is a waste of time."

"Our Great Grandma Elizabeth shot her husband, our Great Grandpa Willard, in the doorway of a cotton house. It wasn't her fault," I explained, "but he died anyway. When she came back here to live, Great Grandma didn't bring money or a treasure."

"She didn't bring it back here," Mary Lou reasoned, "because it was too big to move. It's still at Big Pine."

Even though it was filled with her things, Grandma's trunk wasn't a hope chest, and it really wasn't hers. I didn't have a hope chest but lots of girls did. All the ones I saw were made of cedar and held what a girl thought she might need for when she got married. Turner Furniture used to give girls jewelry boxes at eighth grade graduation. Those miniature Lane chests were magic. They cast a spell, and Randall Turner was the wizard. Girls would smell the inside of those boxes all crisp and fresh like new cut cedar, then drag their mamas down to Turner Furniture to buy huge, expensive cedar chests to fill with totally stupid stuff.

On her birthday, Priscilla Jane Jenkins wanted pillowcases to put in her hope chest. Pillowcases for a hope chest when she didn't even have a boyfriend.

Grandma Rachel's trunk had actually belonged to Grandpa John. It was a big hump back chest covered in leather with wooden slats nailed around the outsides. The lock was like a flattened-out clock hammered onto the front. It looked like a clock but was actually two pieces of metal snapped together in the middle. That trunk had carried all Grandpa owned when he came to D'Leaux. Once he married Grandma Rachel, it sat at the foot of their bed and was filled with her keepsakes. The insides were lined with old yellowed wallpaper and smelled of summer days a long time ago. That trunk had sat in one spot all of my life. Then one day it wasn't there.

Just before Christmas, Ronny Morris got sent to military school in New Mexico. He drove his old car, the one Mr. Morris bought to keep him out of school buses, through the window of the Pic-a-Pac. Ronny thought he could drive through a plate glass window, steal the cash register, then get away before anyone noticed. Herbert Stanley, the town night watchman, noticed right away. He caught Ronny with a crowbar trying to pry loose the cash register from the counter. With or without the cash register, Ronny was going to get caught. Driving through the window busted his radiator.

Ronny could have gone to Marion Institute, but the principal Mr. McCann wouldn't recommend his transfer. "Ronny Morris needs to be as far from D'Leaux as possible,"

Mr. McCann told the newspaper. "Marion, Alabama is too close."

The only place that would take him was New Mexico.

After Ronny left, Mary Lou stopped coming to the house. She decided we lived too far out in the country. Riding back and forth was a big waste of time and gas. Maybe we shouldn't even be best friends; they were moving anyway.

"Ronny Morris' car is still down at the salvage yard," Grady said. "You want to take a look, Little Bit?"

"What for? I didn't even like Ronny."

"I didn't like him either; but come on, go anyway," Grady insisted.

We rode down to A-1 salvage, and the car was sitting out front right by the fence. Mr. Jones who owned the place loved old cars. He had them stacked in piles over an entire hillside. If you let him start, he would talk forever.

"The forty-seven Packard was a fine automobile," Mr. Jones said, running his hand along the roof of Ronny's car. "This Custom Super Clipper has a 128 inch wheelbase. It was stretched out, Grady, longer than pre-war cars."

"Henney Motor Company out of Freeport, Illinois built the chassis for Packard," he went on. "Henney used the best materials. Real quality, made to last."

"Take a look at that interior, Grady," he said. "That's real English broadcloth on the seats, still just like new. No kid should have ever had this car. It's busted, but it's still a beauty."

On the passenger's side, a Scotch Dental Snuff can had rolled out from under the seat and a bunch of old buttons lay scattered on the floorboard.

Grady knew. I knew too.

Ronny Morris had never been to our house. Mrs. Morris always brought Mary Lou and barely stopped.She would roar down our road, sling gravel circling the mailbox, dump Mary Lou by the gate, then fly back to town in a haze of smoke.

So, who showed Ronny where we lived? Who told him about the trunk?

I didn't say anything. I never did.

Early the next spring, Grady shooed the bobwhites out of the barn and into the woods where they belonged. I knew it was time to let them go. But for some reason, I cried and cried.

The *Ami Du Coeur*

Estelle Mitchell, Dr. Mitchell's wife, was Rose's hero. And Rose was my stupid, selfish sister. Miss Estelle taught poise, public speaking, and dramatic expression. Rose took every class.

Miss Estelle was from Virginia but had married Dr. Mitchell when she was in New York. She had danced in the Ziegfeld Follies and lived for beauty, fashion, and sophistication. All the things Rose loved but couldn't find in D'Leaux. Miss Estelle talked about the real world. She had even been to Paris and knew Coco Chanel.

All the majorettes, especially Rose, loved to hear about Miss Estelle's life in New York. She had rich friends and did exciting things because she was beautiful and knew how to act. Male admirers, each new one more handsome than the last, showered her with flowers and gifts every day of the week. People adored her.

Rose could hardly wait to be adored. She was going to Paris, or at least New York, and be a real person in the real world.

"Say 'get' not 'git,' " Rose preached. "And sit up straight at the table. You wouldn't be so ignorant, Cecil McRae, if you learned something. Honestly, you embarrass yourself and you are too dumb to know it."

Rose lived and breathed Estelle Mitchell. She was the absolute authority on everything and everything about her was perfect. She had an *ami du coeur*, and Rose wanted one too.

"All royal, high born ladies in Europe have an *ami du coeur*," Rose explained. "That's a special, favorite person or pet who goes everywhere with their lady and shares all her secrets. Miss Estelle needs someone who likes her for herself not because she's famous. Having an *ami du coeur* makes living in D'Leaux bearable."

Bill was Miss Estelle's *ami du coeur*. He went everywhere she went except to church. Bill was an agnostic. He was also a goat. A goat who wore a vest and chewed tobacco. He rode on the front seat of Miss Estelle's car chewing tobacco and spitting out the window. They took long rides every Sunday afternoon and came back to town covered in dust and tobacco juice.

People put up with Bill on account of Dr. Mitchell. He had come from Germany during the depression and opened a clinic over Odom's drug store. For years he was the only doctor D'Leaux had. Dr. Morgan eventually came, but he was a modern doctor. He only saw people in his office and you had to pay before you left. Dr. Mitchell wasn't like that at all. He went to see sick folks at home and didn't care when he got paid. Miss Eva, Dr. Mitchell's sister, was his nurse. She took care of Dr. Mitchell's clinic.

Miss Estelle took care of everything else.

She put on plays, led discussion groups, and directed weddings. She directed weddings even when the brides didn't want her to. Bill ate curtains and spit on floors. Miss Estelle never noticed. She never even noticed he was a goat.

"When in Rome, Bill. When in Rome," was all she said. Bill would be grabbing a table cloth or climbing over a sofa.

The summer I was in fourth grade, Miss Estelle organized a "Summer Festival of World Cultures." It was like Bible School without Jesus. It lasted two weeks. The last night we had an open house to show off what we had made and put on a talent show. It was really fun except for Rose. Bill messed up her talent.

Mr. Sinclair's old maid sister, Miss Sinclair, taught my class "Venice, the City of Love and Light." I liked it but could never figure out why Venice is so famous. It sits waist deep in water; and to get anywhere people have to paddle around in boats they call gondolas.

We made masks out of paper mache which is pronounced pa-pea-a-mah-shae and is French for "chewed paper." We didn't chew the paper. We used a potato masher. Once a year Venice held the Carnevale di Venezia. It lasted days and days. Everyone wore the masks they had made so nobody knew who anybody else was.

Grady took "Architecture of Ancient Greece." Mr. Holston, who ran the feed store, taught that class. He was there in World War II. He told Grady it was easier to teach the class than convince Miss Estelle he wasn't in Greece to admire the buildings. He was chasing Nazis.

"It's a fact, Grady," Mr. Holston said. "Women do not understand war."

They built models of the Parthenon. That's a famous temple in Athens made of columns without walls or a roof. The Turks blew the top off because they hated the Greeks. Grady used Lincoln Logs for his Parthenon and my Snow White figurine for the statue of Athena that stood in the middle.

15

Miss Estelle taught "Poetry and the Romantics." That was the majorettes' class. They learned poems for the talent show and were the only ones in it. Rose loved Romantic poets. Romantic poets didn't have any money, died all the time, and no one wanted them to get married. Elizabeth Barrett was her favorite. Robert Browning rescued her from her father who had shut poor Elizabeth up in her bedroom claiming she was sick. She wasn't the slightest bit sick. She just wanted to get married.

Romantic poets wrote mostly about plants and animals. Margaret Ann Morgan recited "Daffodils" by William Wordsworth. It was about being lonely wandering around looking for flowers. Euba Hollinghead tried to say "Ode to a Nightingale" by John Keats but it was too long to remember. She said, "Away, away, for I will fly to thee" and sat down. William Blake wrote "Tyger Tyger burning bright." Linda Jenkins said it and Sara Gail Holston recited "To a Skylark" by Percy Shelley. That's a really hard poem to understand.

Rose went last. She had memorized a poem that started "How do I Love Thee?" and pretended to be Elizabeth Barrett locked in her room.

"For your entertainment this evening, I am performing a dramatic monologue," Rose began. "I am in love with Robert Browning and we are eloping tonight. My love will be here soon."

"How do I love thee? Let me count..."

Right then Bill jumped onto the stage like he was part of the talent. He trotted over to Rose, sat down, and spit a chew of tobacco on her shoe.

Rose was really, really mad, but she didn't let on. She didn't even notice Bill. She finished the poem, made a bow, and marched off the stage.

Everybody whistled and clapped to beat the band. Watching Bill spit tobacco was the best part of the program.

Riding home, Grady said, "You're right, Rose. Having an *ami du coeur* makes living in D'Leaux bearable. It really does."

We laughed for days.

The Curse

JT is causing a commotion at Big Pine. It's his. All 6,000 acres are his, his birthright, and he's not leaving.

Big Pine is not his. It belongs to the Windham Presbyterian Church.

On his deathbed, Baxter Sandstrom Willard signed a will to that effect. Grady and Brother Monroe are going up when the weather clears to try and talk reason.

JT is a Willard through his father Chambliss and his grandfather Billy. JT is a Willard. With a Willard there is no reason.

Baxter Sandstrom Willard came to Mounds County in 1845. He poled barges up the river from Mobile with 300 slaves and began clearing the virgin pine forest. He purchased the land from the railroad for five cents an acre and set about building himself a kingdom. Where he got the money or why he chose Mounds County is no more than rumor. Baxter Sandstrom Willard was JT's great grandfather. He was a great grandfather to Grady and me as well. He may have been a friend of Andrew Jackson. Or maybe he was running from a man he robbed in Richmond and left for dead. No matter. He came to Mounds County and never left.

He killed or drove off the few remaining Indians on the property and carved Big Pine Plantation from the wilderness. His fields grew cotton, corn, and rice. The river road took his goods to market and brought back fresh slaves. Before the war, he was the largest landowner in Mounds County and the most successful. He married Elizabeth Dickens in 1851. He was shot in 1879. His son Billy, JT's grandfather, pulled the trigger; but Elizabeth took the blame. Billy was young; his life would have been ruined.

Years later he admitted the truth of that day. Billy was a grown man but he cried like a baby when they carried his mother out of the house to her grave. He had kept his promise; he let his mother take the blame for what he had done.

"Daddy was a hard man," he told Grandma Rachel at their mother's funeral. "He beat us boys like he beat his slaves. The war ended and the slaves ran off. They ran to the North or wherever else they could hide. We were all that was left, his sons and his mules.

"Whenever Daddy went to town—he went nearly every day—he gave us boys jobs to do. If the jobs weren't done when he came home, everyone had to answer. He whipped us with mule traces. Time and time again, he whipped us until our backs ran red."

On that day in October, he had left the boys to haul in corn. Come evening they were still down in the McIntosh field. An axle had broken on the wagon and the boys were using a sled. It was slow, frustrating work. The weather was hot, hot and dry. Not a breath of wind. Gnats swarmed about their heads like thirsty sand, and mosquitoes made misery of any shade. Despite the boys' efforts with coal oil and pine tar, horse flies pestered the mule making her kick. Every kick upended the sled slowing the work even further.

Their mother Elizabeth was sitting in a cotton house on the edge of the field pulling off peanuts. When the boys heard their daddy's mule braying down the path, they headed for the cotton house and their mother. They knew what was coming. The corn was not in.

Billy had the gun. Reconstruction had ended, but times stayed hard. Fear and hatred might drive a man to desperate things. Anyone with any sense kept a gun handy.

Baxter started cursing, calling his sons to come out. To come out and get what was theirs. Swearing even more punishment for their disobedience, he finally climbed up into the cotton house. Billy shot him then and there, square in the gut with a six gauge, double-barreled shotgun. The blast blew his dark silhouette out the doorway shattering the light beyond.

There were five boys: Baxter Sydney, called Billy was the oldest. Then Matthew, Benjamin, and Hugh. Noel the youngest was eleven. Elizabeth took the gun and made the boys swear. And they did.

Great Grandpa Willard didn't die right away. But he did die. They took him over to old Doctor Mozingo's and sent for Richard Adams, an itinerant preacher holding camp meetings at Winslow Bridge. Brother Adams wrote the will on two blank pages from his Bible using a duck feather quill. Great Grandpa scratched "Baxter Willard" onto each page, and Doctor Mozingo along with Arthur Leggett his hired hand signed as witnesses.

"My house, my barns, my lands—all I have wrought from this desolate place—I leave to Windham Presbyterian Church. May it be a light however dim in the gathering dark. I reject, deny and cast out any male claim on what is mine from now unto eternity. Let my sons, the deceitful lazy dogs they are, forage for their food and look with shame upon what they have lost. And to my wife, my loving wife, I bequeath only what lies beneath my lands all the way to the gates of hell where I know she will dwell in everlasting satisfaction."

Black folks say Baxter Willard didn't die. The devil took him. They heard the devil dragging chains in the river calling for him to come out. To come out and get what was his. The chains would drag and the howling begin. This went on day and night while Baxter Willard lay cursing. Cursing his boys, cursing his wife, and they say cursing God. Finally it was over and the howling ceased.

Arthur Leggett left the night Baxter died. For where no one knew. Doctor Mozingo and the preacher were gone within the year. They died. They died suddenly and without warning.

Brother Adams fell from his horse in a fit and choked on his tongue.

Doctor Mozingo dropped dead on the courthouse steps after testifying before the Grand Jury.

He had testified, "Elizabeth Willard was bereft upon the accidental shooting of her husband. She suffers from female hysteria. Considering her age and her condition such hysteria is to be expected."

The will was executed in January of 1880. Elizabeth Willard returned home to her father's house, and the following spring gave birth to my grandmother Rachel Rose. The daughter, because he did not know, Baxter Willard could not curse.

Elizabeth's sons, even Noel, remained at Big Pine unconvinced of their loss. Their father cast them out, but they could not leave.

The Silver Dollars

"Popular hostess Mrs. Dedra Taylor put aside her many cultural interests last Saturday to welcome her cousin Mrs. Rachel McRae of Windham, Mississippi, into her lovely Palmetto Springs Drive home. The two ladies enjoyed a day of laughter and fun remembering their many childhood adventures. Mrs. Elizabeth Britton and children joined the cousins for refreshments before the company returned home to Windham."

—Social Section—*Meridian Star*

Not one word about my birthday.

For my tenth birthday, Mama took Grady and me to the rodeo in Meridian. Grandma Rachel went along to spend the day with her cousin Dedra. I didn't know Cousin Dedra but she was embarrassed. I knew that even as I sat in front of my birthday cake. She was embarrassed, and she made it my fault.

Cousin Dedra was Dedra Horn Taylor, Grandma Rachel's cousin and childhood friend. Her grandfather Esa Horn was brother-in-law to Edward Dickens, Grandma Rachel's own Grandpa Teddy.

As a child, Grandma Rachel rode the train to Meridian and spent several summers with her Horn relatives. It was there she ate ice cream for the first time and saw electric lights.

Esa Horn owned the Meridian Mercantile and one time ran for congress. He didn't win but got lots of votes. His son Benjamin Horn, Dedra's daddy, built a broom factory and made lots of money selling brooms to the army.

My birthday was going to be perfect. I didn't even mind Jerry Jenkins and his sister Prissy Jane tagging along. We had tickets to a real rodeo and Gene Autry would be there. After the rodeo, we were going to Cousin Dedra's house to see television.

The Meridian fairground was huge and packed with people waiting for the rodeo. Trailers and horse pens and tents were jumbled around in no sort of order, and everything smelled like a musty old barn. We could walk around and look anywhere we wanted so long as we stayed together and didn't climb a fence.

A man had buffalo and longhorn cattle in a pen for sale, and for two dollars you could sit on a camel's back and have your picture made. We saw a blacksmith shoeing horses, and a midget cowboy practicing rope tricks.

We looked a long time in a tent stacked full of western stuff: cowboy hats, spurs, tomahawks, Indian headdresses and real Mexican jumping beans. Jerry paid twenty-five cents for two jumping beans in a little red box for Miss Everhart. Miss Everhart was Jerry's Sunday school teacher and had been a missionary in South America.

"Headhunters chased Miss Everhart through the jungle and she barely escaped," Jerry said. "Jesus saved her."

The Jenkinses were Baptists. Jerry and Priscilla Jane were forever talking about missionaries and how hard it was to save savages. Every November, Priscilla Jane gave her allowance to the Lottie Moon offering. You would think Lottie Moon herself personally on her own drove the devil out of China because Priscilla Jane Jenkins sent her fifty cents.

Another tent sold cowboy supplies: saddles and saddle blankets, bridles, stirrups, and all sorts of rope.

"This is the tack tent," Grady said. "That's what a horse needs to do his job. A real cowboy buys the best tack he can afford."

We decided what we would buy for our own horse, then got corn dogs and drinks and found Mama. The rodeo was finally starting.

First was the grand parade. When the rodeo queen rode into the arena, we jumped to our feet clapping and cheering. She wore a glittery gold cowgirl outfit and carried a huge American flag. Then came the cowboys hooting and hollering waving their hats. The parade was like a race. The queen galloped so fast the flag fluttered straight out behind her and the cowboys stayed right on her heels. Around and around they went finally ending up jammed together in the middle of the arena facing the grandstands.

"Why isn't Gene Autry singing "The Star Spangled Banner?" I asked. Some little boy who didn't know half the words messed it completely up.

After the national anthem, the pledge of allegiance, and the prayer, the rodeo part got going. Barrel racing, goat tying, and steer wrestling came first. In between cowboy events Gene Autry sang or the clowns acted silly. My favorite song was "Ghost Riders in the Sky." Mama liked "Buttons and Bows." The clowns had a chuck wagon race but the wheels kept falling off their wagons. One time they tried to make moonshine, but the still blew up covering the clowns with corn mash and ashes. Then they pretended to be drunk. We laughed and laughed.

At the first intermission, Gene Autry stepped to the microphone, "Attention, attention," he said. "I need every cowboy and cowgirl between the ages of six and sixteen to meet me in the arena for some real rodeo fun."

Grady, Jerry and me had the greatest time. Prissy Jane wouldn't go because her shoes might get dirty. We ran sack races, played tug-a-war and threw water balloons. At the end, everybody got a Gene Autry comic book or a dog whistle, the kind only dogs can hear no matter how hard you blow.

"Now Cowgirls," Mr. Autry said, "pick your favorite cowboy and promise him a kiss. At the next intermission," he said, "the cowboys are going to win silver dollars for their sweethearts or maybe bring home the bacon. But ask your parents first, Partners. The going might get a little rough for a tenderfoot."

Grady won ten silver dollars in the calf roping contest and Jerry caught two pigs. The pigs were real slicky. They were greased. Grease wasn't stopping Jerry. He grabbed up the first pig right away then started after the second. It was the funniest thing ever watching fat ol' Jerry Jenkins carrying one squealing pig and chasing another. I was laughing so hard my sides hurt.

When the buzzer sounded, Jerry was sitting in the middle of the arena clutching one pig in his arms with another one clamped between his knees.

"Come on up here, Little Partner," Gene Autry said. "It looks like you got one pig too many."

The crowd roared.

The clowns set Jerry on the stage right next to Mr. Autry. "I had to catch two pigs, Mr. Autry, sir. I have two girls."

"Two girls?" Mr. Autry asked. "Do you have two women you're trying to please?"

The crowd roared even louder.

"Yes sir, Mr. Autry sir. My twin sister Priscilla Jane and my girlfriend Cecil McRae. I like them both."

Mr. Autry turned to the stands and patted Jerry on the back, "Give this cowpoke a big hand, folks," he said. "He's a braver man than I'll ever be."

Everyone was laughing and clapping. Even the clowns were doubled over.

Excuse me, Mr. Autry," Jerry piped up. "Excuse me, sir. Would you do something please?"

"What 'ja need, Partner?" Mr. Autry asked.

"Would you sing 'Happy Birthday' to my girlfriend Cecil McRae? She likes you a lot and she's ten."

It was the best time ever. Gene Autry sang me "Happy Birthday," Grady won ten silver dollars, and Jerry Jenkins gave me a baby pig. Her name was Sylvia. She had a wiggly pink nose, long eyelashes, and sweet little blinky blue eyes. Priscilla Jane didn't want a pig so Jerry traded Grady for five silver dollars.

Then we went to Cousin Dedra's.

Grady, Jerry and me were too dirty for her living room, and the pigs absolutely could not come into the house. They couldn't even be on the porch. Beatrice, Cousin Dedra's help, carried them to the tool shed behind the garage.

"Make sure to lock that door, Beatrice," Cousin Dedra warned.

"Civilized people do not chase swine."

Mama wiped us off on the back porch while Beatrice covered the dining room floor with sheets.

"Filth is death to a nice rug," Cousin Dedra explained.

We washed our hands in the kitchen sink. Then did exactly as we were told: we walked very carefully through the house without touching a thing.

When we were all sat down at the table, Grandma Rachel came walking in with a real birthday cake. It came from the Starlight Bakery on Third Street and had my name on the top. I got the first piece. And we had ice cream.

"What a wonderful day we've all had," Cousin Dedra said right in the middle of my party.."But our birthday girl looks too tired for television. Why don't we save that treat for another time."

My eyes started burning and a lump in my throat got so big, I couldn't swallow my cake.

For the longest time after that, I didn't want to like the rodeo. I felt stupid for getting dirty and for wanting a pig.

"I don't care about dirt," Grady said. "And I like pigs. Pigs are smart. Besides that, Cecil McRae," he continued, "I feel sorry for Cousin Dedra."

"You're sorry for Cousin Dedra, Grady? How could you be sorry. She's mean."

"I feel sorry for her," he said. "And you should too. She's old, Little Bit. She couldn't catch a pig if she wanted to. That's why she doesn't like them. And I know she's never been to a rodeo."

The Christmas Gift

The best Christmas I can remember is the Christmas Grady found the baby. We didn't get to keep him, but saving the baby was really exciting. It was before Grandma died and Rose was still home.

Grady and I found him when we went down below the tanning trough spring to cut our Christmas tree. Selecting the tree was our first official act of the Christmas holiday. We always did that Thanksgiving afternoon. Now the Saturday before Christmas, we were cutting the tree and bringing it home.

There was a story, I don't remember how we knew it, about a very special Christmas. The children in the story needed a tree. Because they had no one to help, the little boy and girl went alone into the forest. It was a snowy winter day, and they were hungry and poor, but they really wanted a tree. When they found the exact right one, they tied a blue ribbon around the trunk to keep it from being cut before they could come back.

Finding the right tree became a ritual of my childhood. Every year Grady and I picked out our tree and tied it with ribbon. We would return later to get the tree just like the children in the story. We always worried about our tree until we actually got it to the house. Would the tree be there when we returned? What would we do if it was gone? In reality, no trees were in danger of being cut except by us. It wasn't cold, and we weren't particularly hungry or poor. But we did what the children in the book did as exactly as we could. Doing things correctly would insure a very special Christmas.

My favorite Christmas trees were cedars. A cedar has bushy limbs to hold lots of decorations and has a nice pointy top just right to hold the star.

Without fail we picked a tree too tall to bring inside. The art of the perfect tree was to trim off just enough to make it fit while allowing the top to still brush the ceiling. One year instead of sawing the tree off from the bottom, Rose sawed it off from the top. She took the perfect pointy part for the star into her room to be her own personal Christmas tree. All her presents had to be under her tree not ours.

"Do you really want to have Christmas by yourself, Rose?" Mama asked.

Grady was all for getting another tree. Then Mama realized the five branches of the topless tree reaching toward the ceiling looked like points of a king's crown. Or maybe the star of Bethlehem shining over the manger.

"Do we really need another tree?" she asked. "This one is so beautiful and so full. But you decide."

We made that entire tree a crown for the baby Jesus. Right at the top, Grady looped gold garland up and down between the five branches. We put icicles all around the sides and used red and gold balls for the jewels. That year was a really good tree.

The year Grady rescued the baby, we were just about to chop down our tree when we heard a kitten. A pitiful little cry came from on down the hill toward the river. Grady saw him first. Not a kitten, the baby. He was sitting in the middle of a logjam right in the edge of the water.

Before I could say a word, Grady splashed into the river. He crawled over the tangled heap, got the baby and climbed back up the bank.

"Somebody lost that baby, Mama. Or do you think they threw him away?" I asked.

Mama called Sheriff Dugger and Doctor Mitchell. They both came to the house along with Miss Hightower. She brought some diapers, bottles and baby clothes.

Miss Hightower was Mama's friend and a member of her ladies' club. She had been my third grade teacher but now worked at the welfare office. She was in charge of babies. Sometimes people have children they don't take care of. Miss Hightower found places for them to live. By the time she got to the house, Mama had fed the baby a bowl of soupy oatmeal and given him a bath. He was swaddled up in Grandma Rachel's arms being rocked by the fire. Doctor Mitchell said the baby was well fed, at least nine months old, and had been in the water more than a day. Other than peeling skin, bug bites, and scratches, he was fine.

"Can we keep him, Mama?" I asked. "Miss Hightower can get him a baby bed and I can roll him around in my doll buggy."

"I live here, Cecil McRae," Rose pouted. "This is my home not an orphanage for discarded infants."

"Are we decorating for Christmas today?" Mama asked. "If we are, Little Bit, you and Grady need to hurry back after that tree."

"And don't bring back any more babies." Rose said.

Sheriff Dugger couldn't find anyone anywhere who had dropped a baby in the river. Heavy rains in Hamilton County to the north of Mounds had washed out roads, but no people had washed away. Miss Hightower brought us a bed and a highchair, but we couldn't keep the baby forever. If his parents weren't found, he would have to go into foster care. That was the law.

"I don't understand why we can't keep baby Mario, Mama," I said. "Grady and I found him. Why isn't he ours?"

"Why are you calling him Mario, Little Bit?" Mama asked.

"You know Mario, Mama, the organ grinder. He turns the handle and the monkey dances around and tips his hat. In the Square. In Mobile. I put a nickel in his cup last Christmas. We've seen them lots of times."

"That's the stupidest thing I ever heard, Cecil McRae," Rose said. "That baby doesn't look like an organ grinder."

"He doesn't look like Mario," I said. "He looks like Mario's monkey. But who would name a baby after a monkey? That's what would be stupid, Rose. Mario's monkey wears a little red vest and little plaid pants. Just like our baby had on. The little hat probably washed off his head in the river."

The vest and the pants. When Sheriff Dugger saw what the baby had been wearing, he knew who Mario was. Not who exactly, but what.

Baby Mario was a Gypsy.

When the sheriff put the word out, Gypsies started coming from everywhere. And they all knew Mario.

His real name was Stefan. His mama was dead, but his daddy was a horse trainer. Baby Stefan had tumbled into the river while his family was washing clothes. One moment the baby was sitting on the bank; the next, he was rolling over and over down the river. They looked one whole day and night and all the next day but couldn't find him.

By Christmas Eve, we had a yard full of cars, campers, and trailers, all full of Gypsies. Everyone wanted to touch Stefan, hold Stefan, and dance with Stefan. Grady and I had a great time. It was like the fair. We ate Gypsy food and listened to Gypsy music. One old Gypsy put on a puppet show. The man puppet kept hitting the lady puppet over the head with a stick. It was the funniest thing ever.

Mama wouldn't let us take any presents, but every time we turned around, one Gypsy or the other was offering us something.

"For you," they said. "Please, just for you."

"Rose," Mama said, "we can't tell people to leave just because they are strangers."

"They steal, Mama," Rose insisted. "I'm going to wake up Christmas morning kidnapped by Gypsies."

Doctor Mitchell wasn't afraid of Gypsies. He knew about them from when he lived in Germany. He spent all day Christmas Eve talking to different Gypsies, examining children, and giving out medicine.

"Gypsies steal chickens, Rose, but they don't steal children." he said. "My Polish grandmother, my Oma, was afraid they would carry my sister Eva and me off, but they never did. Maybe they should have," Doctor Mitchell laughed. "You don't need to be afraid, Rose, just because they're different."

He told us lots of stuff. Gypsies never live in one place; they have their own language. That scares folks. Gypsies have kings and queens but they don't wear crowns. And, Gypsies believe in magic, real magic. Sometimes they pretend to put spells on people who are stingy or mean.

Stefan's daddy got to the house Christmas Eve night. His name was Michael. He had driven all the way from Hialeah, Florida, and cried when Grandma Rachel put Baby Stefan into his arms.

Stefan actually liked Grandma Rachel best. She liked him too. She sang old timey songs and played pat-a-cake with his chubby little hands. Stefan laughed and squealed riding the cockhorse to Banbury Cross and made sweet baby sounds when she rocked him back and forth while he went to sleep.

She used to do that with me too, but I don't remember.

Christmas morning our yard looked like the Vermont postcard Jerry Jenkins gave me. Jerry got to ride with his Uncle Vernon all the way to Maine and back and bought me postcards for my collection. Even though he went in July, the postcard was about winter. And that's what our yard was, a winter wonderland.

Frost covered the ground so thick, it looked like snow, and the sun made sparkles in the grass. Long skinny icicles hung from every tree. I hadn't even heard it rain.

When we went outside to look around, everyone was arguing about Baby Stefan. The Gypsies were packed and ready to leave, but Michael wasn't taking Stefan to Florida. Grady had to keep him.

"The river gave him to you," Michael said. "He's yours now."

They all pleaded and begged. Grady had to take the baby. They wouldn't listen to Mama at all. They didn't care about Miss Hightower or what the law said. It was like we were doing something wrong, not them.

Suddenly Grady said, "What if I don't want Stefan."

Everything got quiet, really quiet.

"What if I think taking a baby from his family is stupid and I won't do it?" Grady asked.

"I cannot tell you what to do," Michael said handing Baby Stefan to Grady, "but if you do not want this precious child, throw him back into the river."

Grady didn't throw the baby in the river. I knew he wouldn't. He walked over to an old woman leaning on the side of a truck. "For you," Grady said, putting Stefan into her arms. "Please, just for you. And don't go throwing him in a river because I don't want him back."

Suddenly everyone was laughing and clapping and dancing around. Kissing and hugging.

The Gypsies left, the icicles melted, and we had Christmas. Grady's best present was a dartboard with real darts. Mine was a thousand piece puzzle of Mount Rushmore. Rose couldn't be happy because she didn't get a ukulele.

"Gypsy magic, Grady," Doctor Mitchell said when he came by later. "You were touched by Gypsy magic."

"I didn't feel magical," Grady said. "That old lady has a rocking chair. The only one I saw. And Stefan loves to rock."

"That old lady was Stefan's Oma, Michael's mother, Grady. You gave the baby back to his family," Doctor Mitchell said.

"Maybe they wanted me to do that, Doctor Mitchell. Gypsies are smart. They're smart enough to get what they want without magic."

"Smart, Grady?"

"Smart, Doctor Mitchell. Really smart. They stayed here an entire week visiting and having a good time. All that while they were getting to know us. They especially got to know Grandma Rachel."

What's smart about knowing your grandmother, Grady?"

"They took the chickens, Doctor Mitchell. Grandma Rachel is too kind hearted to call it stealing. Those Gypsies knew that. All of the chickens, even the roosters are gone," Grady said.

"They got the baby back, Dr. Mitchell, without even talking to Miss Hightower. And the smart part, the really smart part? The Gypsies didn't kidnap Rose."

The Honeymoon

I had never heard the word "honeymoon" until Edna Garrett had one. She married Albert Thompson. That honeymoon transformed Miss Edna. She changed from a certified old maid living with her daddy into a married woman leaving on an exotic adventure, a honeymoon.

I spent an entire summer speculating about honeymoons, weighing the merits of various places I might go and considering how long I had to wait to get one.

Miss Edna taught third grade over in Tuckertown and was my piano teacher. I started taking in second grade. She and her father Mr. Eddie had a big old house on Spring Street and she gave piano lessons in their living room. I walked to their house from school every Monday afternoon. Most of the time I got there before she did and had to visit with Eddie Jr. on the porch. He was Miss Edna's brother. He lived there too but was afflicted. Eddie Jr. was all folded up like he had been on a clothes hanger too long and couldn't straighten out. And, he was all grown but wasn't big enough. Roscoe Washington pulled Eddie Jr. around town in a wagon. He couldn't talk except to say, "Hey, hey, hey," which he said all the time, and he didn't see very well. He wore a pair of binoculars around his neck and looked at close-up things like they were far away. I could never tell what he was looking at, maybe it was me or maybe the porch swing. I just waved like it was me and talked like I thought he had good sense.

Albert Thompson worked for the REA in D'Leaux. The Rural Electric Power Association. If the power went out anywhere in Mounds County, Mr. Albert and his crew got it back on. He had a pig farm and was friends with Mr. Douglas at the elementary school. One January we had a really hard freeze; lots of people were without power. While Mr. Albert was checking the lines, sixty of his baby pigs froze.

"If I can't stay with my sows," he said to Mr. Douglas, "I should get out of the business. Those dead pigs broke my heart."

I didn't realize he even knew Miss Edna until the announcement came out in the paper.

"Mama," I said, "Edna Garrett's picture's in the paper. She's getting married. It says so right here, 'Miss Edna Garrett and Mr. Albert Thompson are presently finalizing plans for their upcoming nuptials.' Did you know that? 'Family and friends are invited through the medium of the press.'"

"The ladies are giving Miss Edna a shower, Little Bit. I'm expecting you to help. Rose and Grady, too."

"Why do I have to read the paper to find out what my piano teacher is doing? 'Guests are further invited to accompany the newlyweds to the bus station to see the couple off on their honeymoon.' Whatever that is."

"It's a trip, Cecil McRae. A very special trip that a bride and groom might take."

38

Miss Edna's party soon took over my life. We had to clean the house even where people wouldn't go, wash all the windows, and carry every scrap of anything interesting or fun down to the barn. We even had to clean Grandma's ferns. Mama had us empty them out onto the ground and wash and paint their pots. Everything had to be party perfect, even those ferns that nobody would look at twice to see or would care about if they did.

The invitations read, "Come join us and celebrate the trip of a lifetime honoring Miss Edna Garrett bride-elect of Mr. Albert Thompson."

The trip of a lifetime! That said it all. Who wouldn't get married for the trip of a lifetime.

"Mama," I asked, "Where's Miss Edna going on her honeymoon?"

"She hasn't said, Little Bit, and it would be impolite to ask."

She might not have said but I knew. If Edna Garrett was taking the trip of a lifetime, she was going to Vienna. That's a city in Austria and the most musical place on earth. Miss Edna loved their music. People in Vienna don't tell stories like "Once upon a time." They play stories. The music makes the words. Miss Edna knew all the "Tales from the Vienna Woods" by heart and played them over and over again.

"If you close your eyes and listen, Cecil McRae," she said, "you might see yourself covered in moonlight twirling around in the arms of a handsome prince. The music says, 'A gentle wind is murmuring in the trees.' Can you hear it?" she asked.

Definitely for sure, Miss Edna was picking Vienna for her honeymoon.

Where would I go? I couldn't decide. When I thought of one good place, an even better place popped into my head.

Jerry Jenkins said he wouldn't marry Miss Edna even if he got a trip to China. Jerry wanted to go to China worse than anything. Charlie Chan always solved mysteries in a flash because he was Chinese. Jerry admitted he could never actually be Chinese, but figured if he got to China he could be as smart. All he had to do was discover the mysteries of the Orient and memorize everything Confucius said.

"When I get back from China," he bragged, "I'll be way smarter than Dick Tracy and twice as famous. Ordinary, every-day-guy Jerry Jenkins will be gone forever. He will have become Mr. Inscrutable."

The shower was really fun. It was all about the trip. The front porch was supposed to be the Greyhound bus station on Court Street. Miss Sinclair and Miss Hightower put posters of famous places like San Francisco and the Grand Canyon on the walls and hung blue and grey crepe paper along the bannisters. Inside, they twisted blue and white balloons into a huge arch around the dining room door.

Grady was the pretend ticketmaster. He stood by the front walk and reminded travelers to watch their step. He was really there to help old ladies onto the porch, but he was not supposed to say so. I was the travel hostess. I opened the front door and asked each guest to please sign the register. I put all the gifts on the gift table and then made sure each guest was invited to have refreshments. Rose was the tea girl. She wore a pair of Mama's white gloves and served punch.

After it was over, Miss Edna gave Grady a slingshot and me a puzzle for being so sweet and helping out. Rose got a box of Magnolia Bath Powder even though she quit serving punch half way through and didn't even pretend to pick up empty plates, which was her job not mine.

The wedding and the reception took place just as the paper had announced. Miss Edna and Mr. Albert married on a Saturday morning in the D'Leaux Baptist Church. Eddie Jr. sat in his wagon right down front and watched the whole thing through his binoculars. After cake and punch in the social hall, Miss Edna, now Mrs. Albert Thompson, changed into her "going away" suit and everyone walked the couple down the street to the bus station.

"You bring her back safe and sound, Young Man," Old Mr. Eddie croaked as they loaded up. The big Greyhound hissed off its brakes, turned the corner, and rolled out of sight.

Walking back to the church, Jerry Jenkins sidled up and whispered, "Hey, hey, hey, I found out where they're going on their honeymoon, Cecil McRae, and it's not Vienna."

"How do you know anything, Jerry. We weren't supposed to ask."

"Roscoe told me. They're going to Mobile."

"Hey, hey, hey, Mr. Inscrutable. What Roscoe Washington knows about honeymoons wouldn't fill a teacup. Miss Edna has never mentioned Mobile much less played a song about it."

"Wanna bet?" he asked. "I bet they're going to Mobile and will be back tomorrow afternoon on the five o'clock bus."

"Okay," I said. "My new Charlie Chan funny book against your silver cat-eye shooter which is mine anyway. Think, Mr. Inscrutable. They can't possibly come home tomorrow. How could the trip of a lifetime last only one day?"

We went to Mobile all the time. Uncle Dewey and Uncle Otis lived there. Once we went at Christmas to see the lights and talked to Santa Claus in the Square. Santa was sitting in a huge gold chair on a stage decorated with Christmas trees, candy canes and giant presents. Everything was all glittery like a pop-up Christmas card with lots of angel hair for snow. Santa talked on a microphone and knew everyone's name; but the presents were fake, just ply board boxes wrapped in reindeer paper. We stood in line forever.

After Santa, we ate parched peanuts and walked around. Lots of stores like Bergman's and Gaucheaux's had gone out of business. They were all boarded up and dark, but the Square itself was a fairyland of lights. We saw Santa only that one time. The next Christmas, he moved to Bel Air Shopping Mall out on Airport Boulevard.

Mobile was fun, but it wasn't the trip of a lifetime.

Monday afternoon, Dumb Ol' Eddie was back on the porch.

"Mama," I asked, "Why would Edna Garrett go to Mobile on her honeymoon and come back the very next day?"

"She hasn't said, Little Bit, and it's impolite to ask."

Miss Edna might not have said, but I knew why her trip of a lifetime turned into a bus ride to Mobile and back. I knew for sure. And I didn't need Charlie Chan to figure it out: Albert Thompson wouldn't leave those stupid pigs.

She should have gone by herself.

Washington D.C.

Until I was grown, Grandpa John was the only man I really knew. He was my hero. Daddy died. No memory, only myth. Mama's brothers Uncle Dewey and Uncle Otis worked in Mobile. They were fun loving, gift givers and game players. Uncle Otis's wife Aunt Cora was unhappy and didn't like us much. At least that's my memory. Aunt Ruby was sickly. Uncle Dewey stayed busy with her. After Robert Earl was born, Aunt Ruby didn't make the trip to Windham, so Uncle Dewey's visits were short until she died. By then he was not what he was. In my mind's eye, he shrank. I know now it was grief taking him away, not his choosing to go. Grandpa John lived and lived. He stayed a long time. He was always old and wobbly, but he stands a giant in my childhood days. Someone who spoke little but saw much, knew everything. Sort of like the wizard in Oz but without the smoke and mirrors.

I loved Grandpa John, but he frustrated my sister Rose. One of Grandpa's pleasures was eating peanuts on the front porch. Rose didn't want him there.

Rose had more boyfriends than the phone book had numbers. She was always getting ready for one or more to show up, and she didn't want Grandpa spoiling the romance. One of the maddest times she ever got was on account of Tiny Boy Busby. Late one evening, Tiny Boy roared up in a '39 Chevrolet smoking more from his nose than his tail pipe. Tiny Boy was captain of the football team; D'Leaux was playing Tuckertown for the district championship; and Rose was "wearing his ring." When he saw Grandpa eating parched peanuts on the porch calmly crunching hulls beneath his rocking chair, Tiny Boy wouldn't get out of the car.

"He eats those peanuts on purpose, Mama. You know he does," Rose complained. "Grandpa does whatever he likes but I can't. Is that fair?"

The romance was spoiled. In fact, it burned rubber escaping back down the road.

Grandpa had one weakness: drinking. He wanted to drink but Grandma Rachel was dead set against whiskey of any kind. It didn't come into the house. Sometimes I caught him in the kitchen slipping whiskey into a glass of water.

"Little Bit," he would say, "Don't go telling your grandma. Every man needs a secret or two."

I didn't tell, but I didn't like it.

As my life unwound from its tiny seed of a shell and grew as nature commands, I came to know Grandpa. More accurately, I came to know his life. His life long before me when he had real secrets to keep. Except for the annual tribute on his grave, he's mostly gone; but he's still a hero and I honor his secrets.

Grandpa John came to D'Leaux as a young lawyer in 1889. He was some cousin to old Mr. McPherson, who Grady's named after. I never knew how, but that connection brought John McRae to Mounds County, Mississippi. It was Grandma Rachel that kept him here. Grandpa set up practice with Mr. McPherson and lived in Mrs. Tinner's boarding house on Davis Street. He was twenty-four, a bachelor, and a graduate of the University of Virginia.

"To the ladies of D'Leaux, John McRae was a star fell to earth ready to light any heart it chose," Mr. Rudolph said. "Miss Rachel, your husband was a fine looking man. No denying that." Mr. Rudolph was sitting on the porch with Grandma paying his respects.

"Within six months of alighting in D'Leaux, Mr. John had sat at every table in town that had chairs and had met every farmer's daughter, sister or cousin in a marrying state of mind. Speculation ran high, and many hearts were looking to their prospects," Mr. Rudolph continued. "You dashed them all, Miss Rachel. You broke a lot of hearts when you said 'yes' to John McRae. He was one smart, fine looking man."

"Pay no attention, Little Bit," Grandma protested, "Mr. Rudolph is telling a tale to ease my heart. He's complimenting me."

What an idea. Grandpa John, young and handsome, sought after. Their wedding picture hung over the fireplace in the front room. That portrait with its black plaster frame fixed in time a stern, solemn man and an equally stern, solemn young woman. Neither the bride nor the groom fit my idea of fine looking.

Our house is just east of Windham, the original county seat of Mounds. Windham's claim to fame was serving for one night as the seat of state government. A marker to that effect stands on the corner of what was then Courthouse Square. The Great Seal of the Confederate State of Mississippi along with the governor and several legislators paused there one night while outrunning the Yankees. After the war, the county seat moved west to D'Leaux away from the river and toward the railroad. Mr. McPherson's law office sat on Station Street just opposite the new courthouse. Grandpa John lived his life between that office and Grandma Rachel.

County folk lived differently from the way we live today. It wasn't until Grandma married that the kitchen was moved inside and the old kitchen became the washhouse. Water came from a huge square hole dug in the ground. Older children drowned in the river; younger ones in the well. I remember once pulling myself up over the railing and peering down into what I thought must be halfway to China. I could see the reflection of the dark water winking back from the bottom and wondered if something lived down there that could come out and get me at night.

In my childhood, we had electricity and a car and rode with Mama to town everyday for school. For Grandma Rachel there was no electricity and no car. School was a mile's walk to Box Corner and going to town meant a two-hour wagon ride Mail came once a week and only then if Mr. Peters thought something worth delivering.

To get things done, Mr. McPherson would ride out to whatever farmer needed his services, conduct the business, then ride back to town. Grandpa John soon took over those duties. Maybe Mr. McPherson was old and tired or maybe he wanted people to meet his new, young partner. Whatever the circumstance, John McRae first encountered Rachel Willard when he rode far out into the county. He went "to witness the last will and testament of one Edward Dickens, a widower and father of Elizabeth Dickens Willard also widowed and living on the property with her youngest child Rachel." Elizabeth Willard was to receive her father's estate without condition or restraint to do with as she deemed fit. John McRae witnessed the signatures, placed the document into his valise and rode back to town. He did those things. But he also fell in love. He fell in love with Rachel Willard. Love of her set his course. She would be his life. But that certainty he locked away. No gesture, no word, no look would betray him.

Love was his secret, a necessary secret. Perhaps one like every man needs.

"The struggle to attract John McRae went on for years," Mr. Rudolph said nodding in my direction. "For some unknown perhaps tragic reason John McRae, like his old cousin Grady McPherson, seemed destined to spend his days in dispassionate solitude, a handsome, but odd man with no interest in marriage." Shaking his head in mock sorrow, Mr. Rudolph concluded, "It was a sad time for the ladies."

"Rudolph Sommes," Grandma interrupted, "I've never known such a doe-eyed notion. John wasn't ready to marry. He couldn't marry. A man needs a living before he needs a wife. And that took a while."

Mr. Rudolph went on, "It didn't take as long as it should have. Mrs. Bates in the Chancery Clerk's office wore completely out. She recorded and re recorded every deed for every property holder in all of Mounds County. For every property holder, that is, who had a love struck female under his roof and was willing to lure John McRae into taking a second look. Always polite and accommodating, John McRae gave good advice," Mr. Rudolph said. "He had nothing else to offer."

"That's nonsense, Rudolph, " Grandma insisted. "You're putting Cinderella notions in Cecil McRae's head. She'll believe fairies live under toadstools if you keep this up."

I would have liked fairies under toadstools, but knew none were there. I did know Grandma Rachel was special. And that 'special' held Grandpa John like Dewey held Bluebell's kittens when they got born under his bed. I wouldn't have called it love. Cocooned in the opaqueness of childhood, I had no name for love, no awareness of love separate from the way things were.

Sometime after Grandpa's funeral, Axle Lackey brought around a load of boxes containing the last of Grandpa's journals and papers. Mr. Axle grew up in D'Leaux and graduated in Uncle Dewey's class. After World War II, like Uncle Dewey, he finished school on the G. I. Bill. He went to Ole Miss and became a lawyer. He started a law practice in Mr. McPherson's old office, but he wasn't Grandpa's partner. I figured that out myself.

Mrs. Hendricks always answered the phone, "McPherson and McRae," even though Mr. McPherson died before I was born. After Mr. Axle came, she started answering, "Law office, Betty Hendricks here."

Grady dragged the boxes up to the attic; and we picked peas and canned tomato chow chow.

That next summer, Grady went off to Washington to be a page for Senator McInnis. He was gone ten whole weeks. I read *Jane Eyre* for the first time and fell in love with Mr. Rochester. Then *Wuthering Heights*. I longed for a tragic lover, some ghostly power blowing back the curtains to possess my soul. I thought of Grandpa and those broken hearts.

The boxes from Grandpa's office were actually wooden crates. Someone had burned "Return to Faxon Peaches, Hancock, Miss." into the sides of each box. I remembered the wood burning set I got one time from Uncle Dewey and wondered if I could ever write that neat with something so hot. I didn't think so. Anyway, Mama put away the burner part of the set after she caught Grady and me burning our names into the wall underneath the kitchen table.

That summer, I read all Grandpa's journals. He sometimes made daily entries but mostly by the week or month. In April 1889, he paid Mrs. Tinner ten dollars in advance for room and board. He paid twelve dollars in May because he added laundry services and a tub bath once a week. In September 1889, he bought a horse and saddle from Jacob Jenkins "...for necessary travel throughout the county, thirty dollars."

He wasn't talkative in his journals, but I came to see him clearly. He was an honorable man, an honorable but helpless man held by one who yet had no name for love. His capture recorded in a fine, neat hand with sparse emotion or embellishment.

October 24, 1889, "...Witnessed and accepted for keeping will of Edward Dickens, Barren Fields, east of D'Leaux. R?"

November 16, 1889, "...Joined Windham Presbyterian Church. R?"

January 16, 1890, "...accepted position as secretary/treasurer WP church. R. Know time, will not be discouraged."

The chronicle of Grandpa's first nine years in D'Leaux included business dealings, court actions, the occasional purchase of clothes, and scant but persistent references to R.

In April 1892, R had high fever. "...caused great worry." In July 1893, R visited family in Meridian. "...home safely on train."

During July 1894, '95, and '96, R attended shaped-note music meetings. "...is there an attachment?"

In 1898, observations turned to actions.

March 12, 1898, "...Easter social WP church R 18th birthday... I may begin."

August 1898, "R...some talk."

Christmas 1898, "R...Chinese box accepted."

March 12, 1899, "R...Asked but was refused."

The word "refused" appeared six times before understanding revealed itself.

March 12, 1901, "Dearest, Dearest R. Yes, I am a stupid fool. I do ask, but never offer."

February 12, 1902, "...Know at last what to offer, dare I hope?"

They married May 29, 1902. By then John McRae was thirty-seven; his beloved R twenty-two.

I cried so much that summer, Mama took the Bronte books to the library and paid me twenty dollars to read *Gulliver's Travels* and draw a map of the places he went.

What did Grandpa offer? The journals didn't say. What did John McRae place before Rachel Willard to give his love a name? That offer, that secret, haunted my summer and can possess me still.

The Piano Recital

Waltz in A Minor by Chopin changed my life. I didn't realize it could, but it did. I was in eighth grade and *Waltz in A Minor* was my recital piece. I liked Miss Edna, my piano teacher. I even liked piano. But I couldn't abide recitals. Nothing about them was fun. Wearing scratchy taffeta evening gowns. Sitting quietly hands folded in my lap. Listening. Smiling politely then clapping for *Go Tell Aunt Rhody* three times in a row. Finally at the end, pretending limeade punch and sugar cookies was the best thing ever. What a useless bother.

"Cecil McRae," Mama said, "Next week at your recital, don't forget to notice Eddie Jr."

"How can I not notice Eddie Jr, Mama. I'll have to step over him to play. Why's he there anyway? That bothers people, Eddie Jr. sitting right up front by the piano looking through those binoculars. Somebody ought to tell Roscoe to move that wagon. You can't depend on either one of them to have much sense."

"After the program, Eddie might like some refreshments, Little Bit. Would you be kind enough to ask?"

There it was. Kindness again. Mama's favorite word. I had to dress like a circus clown, pretend Betty Louise Rankin was special and ever so sweet even though she was in Miss Bledsoe's kindergarten for the second time when she should be in first grade. And to top it off, I had to be kind to Eddie Jr. Eddie Garrett couldn't tell b flat from f sharp much less play a piano.

Why couldn't recitals be fun? Janie Jenkins, Jerry's prissy twin sister, took piano from Mrs. Brister. Janie got to pick whatever music she wanted to learn, and she could play any song she memorized for the recital. She was playing *Stairway to the Stars.* I loved that song. Mrs Brister even said Janie could learn the words and sing along while she played. Miss Edna assigned everything for her students which wasn't really fair. *Waltz in A Minor* was awful. I knew it by heart, but Chopin didn't have words. He was boring and his songs went on and on. They never ended. No wonder he died young. What did he have to live for?

One day after I finished my lesson, Miss Edna leaned forward close to the piano and whispered, "Can you keep a secret, Cecil McRae?"

A secret? How could Miss Edna have a secret? She taught school in Tuckertown. She was married to Albert Thompson. His farm was out near Bells Crossing but she stayed in town with Mr. Garrett and Eddie Jr. What else was there to know?

"It's about Chopin," she said.

"He's dead, Miss Edna. What else is there to know?"

"Mama," I asked later, "Do you think Miss Edna is right in the head? Not as bad as Eddie, Jr. Just a little off?"

"You cannot get out of your recital, Cecil McRae. Miss Edna has not lost her mind. She is an intelligent, responsible woman.

"She's weird, Mama."

"There is nothing weird or strange about Edna Thompson. She is a talented musician. You are lucky to have her as a teacher. To play well, Little Bit, you must trust your teacher. You must believe what she says."

Mama was no help. Neither was Jerry Jenkins. Jerry claimed we were engaged, but he was really just my best friend. Jerry didn't like music.

"I want to find out about Chopin," he said. " I really do. But I can't play the piano. My fingers don't fit the keys."

"That's an excuse, Jerry. Fats Domino is way bigger than you. And he plays the piano just fine."

"As I have often said," Jerry continued ignoring the obvious, "When you have eliminated the impossible, whatever remains, however improbable, must be the truth."

"You do not often say that, Jerry. So stop making things up to sound important. Sherlock Holmes said those exact words to Dr. Watson in *The Sign of Four.*"

'But what if Miss Edna is right? What if magic is real. I mean really real. *The Mystery of Chopin*", it must be solved, Cecil McRae. But how?"

"It's elementary," I said. "To solve the mystery, we follow the clues."

"What clues?"

"Isn't it obvious? The clues are in the music, Jerry. I must trust my teacher, believe what Miss Edna says. I must imagine, I must experiment. I must wander beyond the notes like a blind man. Only then can that magic which never dies fall like fairy dust on all who hear its song."

"Miss Edna is weird, Cecil McRae. Really weird. But weird or not, I'm going to that recital. 'The game is afoot!'"

For one whole week I followed the clues. I practiced the way Miss Edna said. I wandered. I imagined. I played and played. By the time I sat down for my recital piece, Chopin had changed. *Waltz in A Minor* danced around Miss Edna's front room. It was light and airy, delightful and fun. Thrilling. Miss Edna was right. Chopin was alive with possibilities.

I loved my recital. I felt the fairy dust. Everyone did. Even poor Eddie. He heehawed like a donkey. And, I had to bow twice. During refreshments, Albert Thompson shook my hand and called me Miss Britton. Jerry Jenkins decided we were going to Paris on our honeymoon. He wanted to test for magic. Paris had to be full of it because Chopin was buried there. His grave is always covered with fresh flowers and people hang around crying like he didn't die a hundred years ago but passed away unexpectedly one day last week. And Miss Edna is having a baby. She couldn't stop smiling, especially at Mr. Thompson.

After that night, I wondered about Chopin and Miss Edna. Miss Edna wasn't plain and sad any more. She was beautiful and happy. Could Albert Thompson be Chopin? Could he be thrilling? Alive with possibilities? Could a pig farmer be magic? Or was he what I had always thought: without meaning, only mindless notes on an endless page. I wondered but never knew. It was not polite to ask, and Miss Edna never said. It might be a secret.

The Underwear

Until my sister Rose had to have panties, I thought everyone wore step-ins. Rose was getting ready for her senior trip and arguing with Mama about what to take. She had to have Vanity Fair panties. Rose absolutely had to have everything new for her senior trip.

The senior trip was the most important thing about being a senior. Classes worked all through high school earning money. Then just before graduation, the entire group along with their sponsors went somewhere together. Bake sales, car washes, and donkey basketball games were the usual fare. Every class competed for the most money and the best trip. During Grady's junior year, his class held an all male wedding. Everybody in town paid fifty cents a ticket to see Mayor Edward McAdams (the bride) marry Sheriff Charles Dugger (the groom) with Judge Pickering officiating. The reception cost an extra twenty-five cents: cake, punch, and Marvin Newsom being Liberace.

Most of the time, the senior trip was overnight to Nashville and the Grand Ole Opry or maybe to Chattanooga and Lookout Mountain; but Rose's class went to Mexico. It was the most exotic thing ever to happen in D'Leaux. Thirty seniors would travel by chartered bus to Brownsville, Texas, then go into Old Mexico. That year, my sixth grade class went to Mobile. We went and came back the same day. It was really fun, but a tour of Spanish Fort and a picnic in Bienville Square couldn't compare with a senior trip to Mexico.

Margaret Ann Morgan was the real reason the class went to Mexico. Margaret Ann was in Rose's grade, and she got everything. Her daddy, Dr. Morgan, paid for the trip. He gave Miss Sinclair, the senior class sponsor, enough money for the bus and the hotel. All the seniors had to pay for was food.

Margaret Ann was head majorette, an honor just under drum major, which she didn't want. Every time the band went to a football game, we got candy bars and soft drinks handed out by Newt, Dr. Morgan's handiman. Once we were on the bus ready to go, Newt would come down the aisle carrying a big tray with every kind of candy bar in the world. Then he brought down the drinks. I always picked Pay Day and Barq's root beer. Grady liked Baby Ruth and Coca Cola. Rose was a majorette and sat in the back. Sitting in the back of the bus meant you were popular. All the majorettes sat in the back. They ate Zero Bars and drank Dr. Pepper. That's what Margaret Ann liked.

You could never tell by looking, but it killed Rose that Margaret Ann got everything. Rose acted like they were best friends. Poor Margaret Ann. After graduation, she went off to Randolph Macon. Then Dr. Morgan's clinic burned; and he got cancer and died. I don't know what happened to Mrs. Morgan. Jerry Jenkins said she was a drunk. With her daddy gone, Margaret Ann had to come home. She went through nurse's training in Meridian and wound up in Chicago married to a man from Canada. I never heard what he did or if Margaret Ann ever thought of D'Leaux. But Margaret Ann getting everything broke our hearts forever.

"Women wear panties. They don't wear step-in's," Rose proclaimed. "Grandma Rachel can wear step-ins. She's not going anywhere. I'm going to Mexico! Don't you get it, Cecil McRae?"

"I get it, Rose," I said. "You're going to Mexico. But what does Mexico have to do with underwear?"

"Mexico is not America. It's a foreign country, stupid. World travelers do not wear step-ins. Maybe I was born in D'Leaux, but I'm not staying here. Clam diggers, Ship 'n Shore blouses with turned-up collars, and panties. That's me, Cecil McRae. Panties."

The only time I remember Rose crying was when Margaret Ann won Heart Queen for the fourth straight time. Any girl in high school could enter the contest, but being a contestant required hard work. Each contestant had a Heart Jar and one month to get it filled with money. Heart Jars were really just glass gallon jugs the girls decorated with red and white construction paper and taped shut. Money was stuffed through a hole in the lid. Opening the jars once the contest started was against the rules.

The contest ended with the Heart Queen Pageant held around Valentine's Day in the high school auditorium. Tickets were one dollar and the auditorium was always full. The pageant itself had four parts: Contestant and Heart Jar Presentation, Talent Review, Questions and Answers, and finally Heart Queen Coronation.

Mrs. Rainwater, the eleventh grade math teacher, sponsored the money part of the contest. She was the one who talked about not opening the jars.

"Now, Girls, why do we keep our Heart Jars sealed? This is the important thing: the money in your jar is not for you. You are not buying a crown. All the money in all the jars together goes to the Heart Association. Queen contestants are the pretty faces of the American Heart Association. You are encouraging everyone to join with you in the important work of saving lives. A heart attack strikes someone every three minutes. It struck Howard Ramey last year. Judy and Edward don't have a father this year because we didn't get the money collected in time. Just think, you might save someone's daddy.

"Only one person can be queen, but each of us can keep a heart from breaking. The judges will not know how much money is in your jar. I will not know. And you will not know. Do not open those jars."

Of course every girl knew to the penny how much money was in her jar. At least Rose knew. She counted hers every night. Her senior year, she had one hundred seventy-five dollars and fourteen cents not counting checks.

An important part of the pageant was the decorations. Mrs. Hancock hosted The Queen's Breakfast on Saturday morning in the home economics room, then all the contestants decorated the stage. The colors were always red and white and the decorations mostly streamers and cardboard hearts. Rose's senior year, the girls cut an archway in the middle of a huge roll of chicken wire then stretched the entire roll across the back of the stage. When the wire was up, they stuffed the all holes with red and white tissue paper. Rose said it was her idea. When a girl's name was called, she posed in the archway before coming onto the stage. It looked really fancy.

The evening started off with Mrs. Rainwater taking her place at the Heart Jar table.

When she was properly seated, Mr. Hutchins introduced the contestants. Each girl came out wearing her evening gown, walking slowly, holding her Heart Jar sort of like the Holy Grail. All the jars now had huge red hearts pasted on the front so you really couldn't see much of the jar or the money inside—just the heart. As Mr. Hutchins told all about her family, good deeds, and future plans, the girl solemnly carried her jar to the front of the stage, turned slowly, walked to the back of the stage, turned slowly again and walked to the Heart Jar table placing her solemn offering into the waiting hands of Mrs. Rainwater. The serious part of the introduction ended when Mrs. Rainwater accepted the jar. The contestant, relieved of her sacred trust, then turns all smiles to face the audience, walks again to the front of the stage, pauses, turns, and finally exits.

Rose's senior year ten girls competed. The only mess up that year was when Trudy Bledsoe dropped her jar. Glass and money went everywhere. Trudy started crying and wouldn't leave the stage. Eventually, Mrs. Bledsoe got her off; Mr. Sinclair swept up the money; and Ann Mary Bishop presented her jar. Trudy didn't do her talent or answer the question.

Rose tried a different talent every year. In ninth grade she twirled her baton to "Stars and Stripes Forever." In tenth grade she did a ballet dance. Something from *Swan Lake*, which she said was very sad and if I had any feelings at all would cry toward the end. That dance almost never ended. Rose took lessons from Miss Adair who came from Meridian every Monday and held classes in the armory.

"I do not take dancing lessons, Cecil McRae. I attend The Vivian Adair School of the Dance."

Rose took tap, ballet, and expressive movement.

When she was a junior, she did a dramatic reading from *Gone with the Wind*. Rose took oration lessons from Dr. Mitchell's wife, Estelle. Miss Estelle was an expert. For her senior talent, Rose did a piano and flute duet. She took turns with herself playing both parts.

After the Talent Review, everybody had intermission to give the contestants time to change back into their evening gowns. Intermission was the best part of the program. The Heart Committee served punch and cookies in the library. While we had refreshments, Mr. Hutchins handed out heart attack papers and Mrs. Rainwater talked with mothers about next year's contest.

"Just look at you, Cecil McRae," she said fluttering around like a drunken chimney sweep, "It won't be long until you outshine your pretty sister. I can't wait to see you up on that stage."

Mrs. Rainwater was as flimsy as an empty flour sack and twice as senseless. When I was in second grade, her husband Harold Jr. stepped on a downed power line during deer season and of course died. Ever since then besides wearing black, Mrs. Rainwater pretended electricity didn't exist. She wouldn't eat anything cooked on an electric stove, wouldn't turn on lights, or run a fan.

"Mrs. Britton," she said swooping in toward Mama, "Cecil McRae will be Queen for sure."

The last two parts of the program ran together and were really short. Mr. Hutchins introduced each girl again for a final walk, but this time the queen candidates stayed on stage lined up for Questions and Answers.

Questions and Answers constituted the poise part of the program. All the questions were silly and we were supposed to laugh. The contestants were judged on how well they responded. Rose worked for days on answers she might give.

"Miss Sarah McBride, please step forward," Mr. Hutchins said and winked at the audience. "Miss McBride, this is a math question. Are you ready?"

"I think I am."

"Miss McBride, your Heart Jar looked mighty full. If it takes two cups to fill a pint and two pints to fill a quart, how many kisses does it take to fill a gallon jug?"

Everybody laughed and clapped.

Sarah started scrunching up her face biting her bottom lip. It was obvious. Sarah McBride didn't have poise.

We finally settled down for the answer, "I didn't think about kisses, Mr. Hutchins. I just wanted money."

The audience roared.

"Miss Rose Elizabeth Britton, please step forward. Your question concerns geography, Miss Britton. Are you ready?"

"Yes, Mr. Hutchins, I am ready."

"This is American Heart Association month, Miss Britton, and every young man in the audience tonight wants you and only you to answer this question: Where is Rose Elizabeth Britton's heart?"

Rose was really poised. She stood perfectly still smiling to beat the band. After just a minute, she cocked her head to one side and in a voice just like Vivian Leigh answered, "Why, Mr. Hutchins, don't you know? My heart is in San Francisco where I long to be."

Then all glamorous and beautiful, Rose turned, curtsied real low to the audience, and went back to her place in line.

That was a great answer. We all clapped and clapped. Everyone knew about Tony Bennett and loved that song. The D'Leaux radio station WDLM played it all the time. Rose had won poise hands down.

Rose ranted and cried for days after Margaret Ann won that fourth straight time. The contest was fixed. Margaret Ann cheated. Nothing in D'Leaux was fair. People who cheated her, and they knew who they were, would be sorry. She wasn't going to the junior/senior prom. She wasn't going to sign yearbooks. She wasn't going to the senior banquet. And she wasn't speaking to Eunice Rainwater ever again.

Rose did go to the prom; she did sign yearbooks. She went to the senior banquet and read her speech that won the American Legion Award. Rose did everything she said she wasn't going to do except speak to Mrs. Rainwater. She wouldn't even look at Mrs. Rainwater, much less speak. But after the contest, Rose wasn't the same. She didn't complain at supper and didn't refuse to take her turn washing the dishes. She didn't even claim the front seat riding to town. She got mad only once and that was with Grady. He wouldn't be in Miss Vivian's dance recital.

Rose needed a male partner. All Grady had to do was stand on stage looking jealous while she did her Gypsy dance then pretend to shoot her so she could twirl around and die in his arms. He didn't have to dance at all, but Grady wouldn't do it.

"I'm not wearing panties, Rose. I've seen how men dancers dress: colored stockings, girlie shirts, and panties. Men dancers wear panties. You can die all you want," Grady said, "but I won't be there."

Miss Vivian's friend Leon played the jealous boyfriend part. Rose was a real star. She twirled and twirled, finally dying in Mr. Leon's arms. Margaret Ann didn't take dancing.

When the seniors left for Mexico, half the town turned out even though it was five o'clock in the morning. Only twenty-seven seniors actually went. Tiny Boy Busby had joined the Army and gone off to camp; and Judy Davis and Evelyn Jones were already married. Miss Sinclair said they didn't want to go.

The bus went all the way to Brownsville, Texas, the first day. After spending the night, the group crossed into Mexico. Stacking their luggage in the lobby of The Royal Palm hotel, the class left for the Spanish market and their first taste of foreign lands. They were to stay two nights in Matamoras, then go to San Antonio, Texas, for a final night before heading home.

Check-in for The Royal Palm was four o'clock. Rose and Euba Hollingshead didn't show up for check-in and their suitcases were gone.

Everyone was in a panic. No one had seen Rose and Euba after the bus ride to the hotel, and no person or group was demanding any kind of ransom. After three days, Euba finally called her daddy. She didn't know it was so far to California, had spent all of her money, and was too scared to hitchhike any further.

Rose had left Euba at a Dairy Queen in Tucumcari, New Mexico.

According to Euba, Rose had over three hundred dollars. She was headed to California no matter how far it was and was never, ever coming back.

We waited and waited for Rose to call.

In D'Leaux, having a secret was an important part of childhood. A secret was what you had that no one knew about. It was the most special thing a person could have. My secret was in a quart jar buried beside the chimney under the house. Grady's was in a Prince Edward cigar box hidden under a rafter in the corn crib. I wasn't supposed to know that but I did. The quickest way to lose a friend forever was to find their secret. My secret was a tiny airplane Uncle Dewey brought, five red jacks from a set I once had, and a whistle Jerry Jenkins said was magic. I don't remember the other things; but at the time, that jar held my most private treasures.

Rose found my secret.

Sometime after she left, after neighbors stopped bringing food, I crawled under the house to hide and play with my secret. The jar was dug up and all my things scattered around in the dirt. And my money was gone. My thirty-four dollars and sixty-six cents hidden with my secret was completely gone.

It was Rose. Grady would never touch a secret. Who else even knew for sure I had one? Everybody thought Euba was lying or stupid to think Rose had three hundred dollars. I knew better. Rose took my money; and what's more, she took her Heart Jar money. That's why she counted it all the time and then wouldn't look at Mrs. Rainwater. With what she took from me and from her Heart Jar plus the one hundred dollars she wheedle out of Mama for food and souvenirs, she had at least three hundred dollars. Rose could get to California. With all that money, she could get to California then some.

Rose wasn't coming back. I knew that for sure. How could she.

I saw Euba down at Mitchell's Dry Goods the other day. She's clerked there for years and knows every bit of gossip to be had in D'Leaux. I didn't go for gossip. I went for panties. They didn't have any. All they had was briefs.

The Cats

Wi'nell Beasley showed up at Lottie Mae's the summer before I went into sixth grade. She came riding up with Grady from somewhere deep in the woods below the Indian mounds. Lottie Mae's little house stood about a hundred yards from our back porch behind a patch of horse chestnut trees. The house had been empty and sad since she died, but it couldn't have been happy to see Wi'nell Beasley. Three old mattresses, a bedstead, two dilapidated sofas, some broken chairs, four wild haired girls, a mute son, and three croker sacks full of cats. It looked like a junk parade gone haywire.

Wi'nell took up the entire cab of the truck. She must have weighed three tons and didn't attempt to move herself until Grady and James John, the boy, had hoisted a sofa onto the front porch. With the sofa in place, Wi'nell emerged from the truck wheezing and coughing like an asthmatic buffalo, shambled up the steps, and collapsed onto the wreckage.

No one seemed surprised except me, "Mama, what's going on with those cats?"

"I don't know about the cats, Little Bit, but the girls don't have a place to live. I thought you might get them ready for school."

"No place to live? Where did they come from? Don't they live there?"

"Their daddy is dead, Cecil McRae, and their mama needs help. They're staying here while things get sorted out."

Wi'nell Beasley was actually Winnie Nell Daily. I got that from the paper. She was the common-law wife, which I knew meant "not married," of Burford Beasley who was dead; and his brother Hershel (Herky) Beasley was standing trial for the killing. The paper didn't mention the children. But there they were hanging around the truck like startled goats.

Grady unloaded the truck; Mama let loose the cats; then Miss Hightower showed up with fried chicken and pimento cheese sandwiches for their supper. That was it. The Beasleys were moved.

Early the next day we left to take Grady to Mobile. He was working with Uncle Dewey all summer loading scrap metal for Japan. Grady got to drive the biggest machine I had ever seen, a giant scoop that lifted scrap from a mountain of rubble and dropped it into a box that was then loaded onto a ship. The scoop was way bigger than a log truck; bigger even than the roller machine Danny Beauchamp's daddy drove to build highways. Danny said his dad flattened an entire house one time with stuff still in it. Nobody was in the house; they got out. But it sat on the right of way and had to go. Mr. Beauchamp turned that house into toothpicks without breaking a sweat.

The silver metal hat Grady wore had his name written on the inside and was his to keep.

When I got a B.O. Plenty doll for my birthday that next October, I was sure Grady loaded the tin that went to Japan to make my doll. B.O. Plenty was a character in Dick Tracy, the best comic strip ever. My B.O. Plenty was holding Baby Sparkle in his arms, and when I wound him up, he waddled back and forth just like he was rocking her to sleep. As he rocked, his insides ticked. The whole thing was magic.

That summer, Grady loaded tin and I worked on Sharon, Bonnie, Evelyn, and Bitsy. They had no clothes other than pieces of old dresses, no shoes or underwear, and their hair had never been cut or washed. Wi'nell and James John looked better off and wore real clothes, but the girls had nothing. I later learned Wi'nell and James John made frequent visits to East Mississippi Mental Hospital in Meridian. The haircuts and clothes came from there. Another thing I learned was Wi'nell didn't want clothes, no matter how good or how big they were. She would just as soon be naked as eat a potato.

Miss Hightower, Mama's good friend, brought by a box of stuff they might use along with some sheets and towels. Mama told me to sort through things and help the girls learn to bathe and take care of themselves. They didn't know a single thing about being clean.

The first thing I had to do was cut everybody's hair. Then I showed each one of them how to take a sudsy bath. Lottie Mae's had only a spigot in the kitchen so I used our bathroom. Mama didn't mind in the least. After we were all bathed and dressed in clothes that fit, we cut our nails, then brushed our teeth. Our bathroom was walled off on one end of the back porch. I set up a beauty parlor on the other end. We spent entire afternoons learning to be clean and making ourselves pretty. We could cut hair and fingernails anytime we wanted so long as the scissors stayed on the back porch.

Sharon and Bonnie didn't talk much but caught on real fast. Once they learned about laundry, they washed all the time. Our wash house had hot and cold water on the inside. They could run the machine in no time at all and really loved putting things through the wringer. We washed all summer. Sharon was the leader and soon had Lottie Mae's house looking as neat and tidy as a pin.

Sharon was also the one who bossed Wi'nell and made her get out of the bed. Once we had four beds put up in the house with sheets and bedspreads, Wi'nell spent her days moving from bed to bed. Honestly, she couldn't do anything; and if Wi'nell could have done something, she wouldn't have. She was too simple to think it up in the first place. Sharon decided Wi'nell had to stay on the porch during the day. She was not allowed to lie in Sharon's nice clean beds.

Evelyn talked up a storm but didn't make any sense. She needed watching every minute, especially around the machine. She put stuff in the washer that didn't belong like an old shoe or a purse. The worst thing she ever washed was Bitsy's cats. We came back from hanging out a load of clothes at Lottie Mae's and found kittens swishing back and forth in the water. Two were drowned. Bitsy was hysterical.

Bitsy could talk but was really too little to do much. She was probably four and Evelyn maybe seven. All the cats belonged to Bitsy. Each one had a different name no matter how many there were, and Bitsy talked to them just like they were people. Darlene and Katy were dead as gnats. Bitsy didn't know about being dead. I told her as plain as day, but she wouldn't understand. She screamed so hard for those cats to wake up I thought she was having a fit.

Mama agreed with Bitsy. The kittens weren't really dead. What they needed was the doctor. Why two dead kittens needed Dr. Mitchell was beyond me, but Mama put them into a shoebox and drove off to town. Bitsy was happy. The doctor would make them well. Bitsy never lived a minute without holding a cat. Cats were babies and needed constant care.

Sometime during the summer, noise started coming from Lottie Mae's. Our house sits at the end of the road. We didn't hear people sounds unless we made them ourselves. Night after night, I'd hear folks hollering and engines roaring. Somebody could drive to Lottie Mae's without coming by our house if they knew to follow the wagon road through the woods. That's what was happening. Laughing and hooting would start about dark and go on for hours. Then one night, I stepped on Sharon and Bonnie. They were sleeping on our porch in front of the bathroom door.

"Mama, something's going on at Lottie Mae's. Do you think James John is trying to drive? I keep hearing a car over there at night. And last night Sharon and Bonnie slept on the porch."

"Maybe they were hot, Little Bit. You like to sleep on the porch when it's hot."

"It's our porch, Mama. Just because we have a screened in porch, doesn't mean anybody who's hot can sleep there."

"Can Sharon and Bonnie sleep on your porch, Cecil McRae? Can you be kind when you don't have to be? Kindness will go a long way if you let it."

I just shut up. Nothing I said was getting Sharon and Bonnie off the porch. Kindness. Kindness was Mama's favorite subject, and anytime it came up, I lost. I had to be kind when Alice Turner broke my China baby doll's head off even though I knew she did it on purpose. I had to be kind when Prissy Jane Jenkins didn't invite me to her birthday slumber party. But I had to invite her to mine and then pretend I was glad she came. I even had to be kind when David Dugger called me donkey face and heehawed all around Mrs. Reynold's room and then did it again on the playground. Now I couldn't even sleep on my own porch. I had to be kind to the Beasleys. I had gone from helping the Beasleys to being kind to the Beasleys. Being kind wore me out.

Miss Hightower checked on things almost every week. Part of her job at the welfare office was looking after children. She was really good at it.

Sheriff Dugger, David Dugger's uncle, was running for re-election. He came around pretty often campaigning. One day when Mama wasn't home, he came by and gave me a fan. It was made of thick, stiffish white paper and stapled to an extra big popsicle stick. "I'm a fan of Sheriff Charles Dugger" in big blue letters covered most of the front. All the fans I had seen before were from the funeral home and handed out at homecoming. They mostly showed pictures from the Bible, Jesus praying in the garden, the empty tomb with a bright light shining from the inside—that sort of thing. My favorite one was the angel helping the little boy and girl over the rickety bridge. Sheriff Dugger left a fan for Mama and said for her to call just anytime.

The noise got so loud at Lottie Mae's I absolutely couldn't sleep, much less go to the bathroom. Sharon and Bonnie practically lived on the back porch.

One thing I never understood about kindness: it was barely mentioned around Grady and had never even come up with Rose. But me, I couldn't eat a biscuit without Mama telling me to be kind.

70

Grady came home the week before school started. He missed the first full week of band practice but didn't get demerits for being absent on account of his job. Grady played trombone. He and Tommy McGinness played first chair, except Tommy had some sort of brain problem. He passed out if he got too hot. One time he fainted in the middle of a parade in Moss and wet his pants. Everybody saw it. It was awful. I was extra kind to Tommy. He couldn't help it.

Mama had to take Grady's band pants up in the waist and let them out in the legs. He looked like a boney brown stick.

"How come you got so skinny, Grady?" I asked. "Didn't Aunt Ruby cook?"

"Working the docks is a hot job, Little Bit. I've been eatin' like a horse, but sweatin' like a Chinaman in a laundry."

Mama just bristled. "All people sweat, Grady," she said, "and there's nothing to disrespect in honest work, even in a laundry."

"Mama," I protested, "Charlie Chan says that sort of stuff all the time, and he's Chinese."

"Grady is not Charlie Chan, Cecil McRae. And neither are you."

We were sitting on the back porch; Mama finishing up Grady's cuffs when just like clockwork the noise started.

"Mama," I complained, "I just don't get it. We've got racket all night; I'm kicked off my own porch. Now, we can't talk about the Chinese."

Mama went on like I hadn't said a word. "Herky Beasley's out on bail. Those girls surely don't need another killing."

"Herky Beasley! Why did Sheriff Dugger let him out?" I asked. "Is Herky Beasley wandering around Lottie Mae's with a gun?"

"One day next week," Mama continued as if we weren't going to be murdered, "Miss Hightower is coming by for the girls. Little

Bit, you could help them get ready if you would. They're going to stay with Mrs. Poe over in Tuckertown."

Two loud booms went off one after the other. Then I realized Grady was gone. Everything got real quiet. So quiet even the trees didn't breathe.

Suddenly, Lottie Mae's sounded like the Daytona Five Hundred. Engines roaring, people shouting, brakes squealing.

Before the dust could settle, Grady was back on the porch. He slipped Grandpa's gun back behind the glider, then cool as a cucumber walked into the house to try on his pants.

Bitsy could take only two cats to Tuckertown so I carried the left-over babies to band practice. The band needed to practice being kind. Kindness had a long way to go in D'Leaux and taking a cat would get it started. Everybody had to choose at least one even Mr. Sinclair, the band director.

Nobody talked back, not even Prissy Jane. She and Jerry took three: Gracie, Maxine, and Peas Pottie.

Riding home with an empty box and no more Beasleys, I dared to ask, "Grady, were you going to kill Herky Beasley?"

"Gosh no, Cecil McRae," he said. "I wouldn't hurt a fly. I shot straight up over the trees."

"But, you acted so normal, Grady. Like shooting at somebody who might shoot you back was like pouring water from a dipper," I said. "Weren't you scared?"

Grady stopped the truck, then looked at me with the most serious face ever. "Don't tell Mama, Little Bit," he said; "But I was sweatin' like a Chinaman in a laundry."

We laughed and laughed. It was the funniest thing ever, but Mama never knew.

The Kidnapping

E ven though she was rich, Edwina Murray looked like a bag of rags. She was a hobo. She lived her life jumping rails riding trains. On the train she was nameless. But in Mounds County, Mississippi, Edwina Murray was famous. She was the only person in D'Leaux ever to be kidnapped.

Not once but twice. Edwina Murray was kidnapped twice.

She sometimes slept behind our washhouse and Grandpa John gave her money from a tin box in his desk drawer. It was her money. Levi Abraham, Edwina's grandfather, was the only Jew in Mounds County and he owned the bank.

She first disappeared off her grandfather's porch when she was two years old. Edwina simply disappeared. She was there one minute and gone the next.

The day before, an Indian woman had purchased a large fancy doll from the D'Leaux Emporium. She was later seen driving a buggy south on the old river road. The buggy was found abandoned at Toufet Crossing; but like Edwina, the woman and the doll were gone.

Mr. Levi knew who had his granddaughter. Everybody did. But no one knew where she was.

Grandpa John and Mr. McPherson figured it out and got her back.

Alfred Murray kidnapped Edwina. He wanted Mr. Abraham to give him money. Mr. Levi wouldn't do it; so Edwina went missing.

Alfred Murray was Mr. Levi's son-in-law and Edwina's daddy. He was a Baptist, but he fell in love with Mr. Levi's daughter Lily. Alfred Murray wanted to marry Lily Abraham so badly he became a Jew.

Mr. Levi finally let them marry and Alfred went to work at the bank. After Edwina was born, Alfred decided he didn't like being a Jew. He didn't like working at the bank either. He wanted to be a businessman and get rich investing in the railroad. When he couldn't have what he wanted, he got mad and left town.

Not long after, Edwina disappeared.

"Alfred Murray didn't really want Edwina," Grandpa said. "He wanted money. That's how we found him, with money."

McPherson and McRae Attorneys at Law printed notices in newspapers all across the South offering a reward for news of Edwina Murray. Five thousand dollars. The exact amount Alfred Murray had demanded months earlier from Mr. Abraham. He hadn't gotten what he wanted then. Maybe now he thought he would. The notices went out week after week, month after month.

"Patience takes a while," Grandpa said, "but it pays off."

After almost a year, the law office received a letter instructing McPherson and McRae to leave the five thousand dollars with the desk clerk at the Admiral Semmes Hotel in Mobile. If their correspondent encountered no difficulties, interested parties could expect news of Edwina. For assurances, the letter enclosed a picture of Edwina holding a huge doll.

Grandpa left the money in a black valise at the desk of the Admiral Semmes as the letter instructed; and Bigman McDougle, Corrine Toufet's brother, and his son Hero started watching the hotel doorman from across the street at the Dixie Gentleman's Barber and Bath. Patience took a while.

After three weeks of doing nothing but opening and closing the big wooden doors of the Admiral Semmes Hotel, the doorman retrieved a huge white kerchief from his pocket and began beating his uniform like a man covered in ants. That was the signal. Bigman followed the woman coming out of the hotel and Hero rode the train back to D'Leaux.

Now everyone waited.

Bigman had two hundred dollars in his shoes and postcards in his pocket. If the five thousand dollars left Mobile, he would know where it went. Bigman McDougle lived on the tracks jumping rails, riding trains. He came home only now and then to earn a little money or maybe see his wife.

Ten days after the money left the hotel with a foreign looking lady wearing a black lace dress and a hat with fancy feathers, a card arrived. The postmark read Galveston, Texas.

"How did you get Edwina back, Grandpa ?" Grady asked.

"They stole her back, Grady," I explained. "That's what they went for. They followed Alfred Murray to his hideout, waited until he was sleeping, then rescued Edwina."

"Stealing Edwina wasn't part of the plan, Little Bit," Grandpa said. "And there was no hideout. Alfred Murray was passing himself off as a widower, an upright citizen, working at the Texas Bank and Trust. He was a member of The Calvary Baptist Church and had even obtained membership in the Loyal Order of Moose."

Grandpa continued, "We went before the Galveston County Court and filed a child custody petition on behalf of Lily Murray. We were waiting for the hearing when Edwina went missing again. She simply disappeared."

"Then, you did steal her. Didn't you," I said.

"We didn't steal Edwina, but the good citizens of Galveston thought we had. A lynch party met us at the courthouse."

"A posse?" Grady asked. "A real posse like in the wild west?"

"A real posse, Grady, with a real sheriff and a real rope. I thought we were going to hang. I could feel the noose tightening around my neck," Grandpa said gripping his throat. "Lucky for me, Mr. McPherson had other ideas. When he eyed those Texans crowding into the courtroom, that judge glaring down from the bench, Grady Alphonso McPherson took control of the proceedings."

Grandpa continued, "I was Grady McPherson's friend and law partner; I knew him to be a brilliant litigator, the best I had ever seen. But his performance in that courtroom amazed even me." Grandpa shook his head, "Those Texasans didn't stand a chance."

"Mr. McPherson rose solemnly from his chair and addressed the bench. 'Your Honor,' he said bowing slightly toward the judge,'Before we begin the proceeding today, may I ask for a word of prayer?' Before I could consider what was happening," Grandpa continued, "the judge banged the gavel for quiet, then stood.

"Hats came off, shuffling stopped, and Mr. McPherson began to pray. He prayed the whole sorry story of Alfred Murray, how he was a Baptist, became a Jew, and married Lily Abraham. Edwina, the doll, the abandoned buggy, anything and everything not allowed in an open court, Mr. McPherson lifted to heaven. The newspaper notice, the picture, the ransom demand, and finally the five thousand dollars carried from the Admiral Semmes Hotel to Alfred Murray's house," Grandpa laughed. "It was the best prayer ever prayed. Jonathan Edwards couldn't have done a better job."

"But what happened? What about Edwina and Alfred Murray?" Grady asked. "And the money?"

"The petition was granted, Grady. Case closed. Court dismissed! The judge awarded Lily Murray sole custody of her daughter Edwina, and gave Alfred Murray thirty days to pay Levi Abraham five thousand dollars or face charges of kidnapping and extortion. And, he had to pay court costs."

"Edwina, Grandpa, what happened to Edwina?" I asked.

"Edwina was fine. Bigman had her, Little Bit. Alfred Murray's lady friend had put her on a train headed for Mexico. Bigman had sneaked her off and hopped the Northern Limited to Chicago."

"Bigman kidnapped Edwina? Why would he do that? Trains are dangerous." Grady said.

"Not kidnapped exactly, Grady. He was keeping her safe. No harm would come to Edwina with Bigman McDougle. And she was happy. Bigman sent postcards from all over. Edwina loved trains."

"They did come home. Didn't they? They had to." I said.

"Yes, They came home, Little Bit. When they ran out of money, Bigman brought her home. But she didn't stay. About the time most little girls start jumping squares in hopscotch, Edwina was jumping rails, riding trains. She came home only now and then for money and postcards."

She wandered so long, all that was left of the Abraham name was the German candy box in Grandpa's desk. The pictures and fancy gold writing were all worn off and the hinges rusted. When Edwina died, Grandpa went to St. Louis to claim her body. Mr. Levi had been dead for years. When the bank got sold to Emmett Jackson, Lily Murray left D'Leaux. Someone said she went down to Florida. I never knew that for sure, but Grandpa John kept charge of Edwina's money until the end.

Grandpa buried her with the McDougle's out at Mount Ebo. He thought that fitting. The last of her money bought the marker and her grave bears testament to lives who pass by but move on. A spoon, the odd can, sometimes a railroad spike appears on her place. People want to say the grave is haunted. It's not haunted, just restless. Her heart is on a train.

The Doughnuts

Irene Willard never acknowledged in any way that her father Matthew Willard, my Grandma Rachel's brother, lost the Ford dealership in D'Leaux. Cousin Irene kept her head high, talked like "Daddy" died only last month, and held desperation at bay for years. She did feel desperation; I saw the abyss, felt its pull, and like her buried it deep for many years.

Being my Great Uncle Matthew Willard's child, Cousin Irene was actually my mother's first cousin. But, she was nearer Grandma Rachel's age and her lifelong friend. I never knew Uncle Matt or his wife Aunt Lydia, but I did know Cousin Irene. She inspired fear and awe in everyone she met, especially me.

In 1904 as a young woman, Cousin Irene left D'Leaux. She went first to Chicago and worked at Kress's Five and Dime. Later she moved to Florida and served many years as a waitress in fancy hotels. Her real life was always away from Windham. Mounds County rated only occasional visits, obligatory and short.

In 1943, Cousin Irene finally came home and stayed. She built a little house next to Cousin Cynthia and Cousin Noel, Uncle Matt's two other surviving children. She cared for Cousin Cynthia and

Cousin Noel until they died and sold vegetables from the trunk of her car. We never got to eat any of her vegetables or ride in any of her cars. Children were messy creatures best kept away from things too nice to ruin.

"Cecil McRae, don't touch that door handle. That automobile is new and you are far from clean."

She got her cars from Mangum Ford, a new one every year.

Mr. Mangum wasn't from Mounds. I don't know the year, but Mr. Mangum moved to D'Leaux and bought the old Ford building from the bank. When he opened the new dealership, no one had sold Ford cars in Mounds County since Uncle Matt had died in 1929.

I liked Mr. Mangum. He always acted glad to see Grady and me and was never too busy to talk. Every year in September, Mr. Mangum held an open house to show off the new models and give things away free.

That's when Cousin Irene got her car. Grady and me would walk over to the Ford place after school to get free doughnuts and two blue and white pot holders for Mama. They stuck to the stove with magnets and said, "Mangum Ford-From Our Family To Yours!" One year Mr. Mangum gave Grady a tape measure no bigger than a silver dollar. The measure part rolled in and out of the shiny silver case like magic. I got a blue and white tin box of Ford pencils with their own little sharpener. I couldn't understand why every kid in D'Leaux wasn't there. Open house day at the Ford place was too good to miss.

Ten or twelve townspeople would be milling around. We would get a cup of coffee from the big pot borrowed from the Methodist church, eat doughnuts and wait. Mostly, we just wanted doughnuts. They were from Shipley Bakery in Mobile. Mr. Mangum had them sent up special on the bus.

About four o'clock Cousin Irene would swoop in, look over the five or six new models on the floor, point in what appeared to me a random selection and say, "I'll take that one, Whitney."

"Yes, Ma'am, Miss Irene," Mr. Mangum always said. "I'll wrap it up and have it ready first thing in the morning."

With that, Cousin Irene could suddenly notice Grady and me.

"Cecil McRae, Grady McPherson, are you two eating Mr. Mangum's doughnuts? Don't you know those doughnuts are for people buying cars? Mr. Mangum is not in the business of giving away free doughnuts!"

I didn't know until Cousin Irene died that Mr. Mangum gave away more than doughnuts. He gave away cars.

The burial was at Windham Presbyterian Church. Cousin Irene lay at rest by her sister and brothers.

That fall, Grady was a freshman at State. I was lonelier than I had ever been in my life. I was like a marble in a cigar box—free to roam but no reason to roll.

One day in early October, I found Grandma in the back room looking through her old papers from her bureau. "I need you to do something, Little Bit," she said. "Tomorrow after school stop by the Ford place and give Mr. Mangum this remembrance of Cousin Irene." She handed me some old pictures and a small pack of letters tied with a strip of faded sacking. "He would like to have these."

I despised Izetta Beasley. Even though she was the only educated Beasley in Mounds County and now she's dead, I still can't like her. She taught my eighth grade English class and sponsored eighth grade. I also had her for last period study hall. Every time I turned around, she was after me.

One day she read the first sentence of my six-week report then lectured the class about plagiarism.

"I didn't say you copied, Cecil McRae. I said plagiarism is the most serious error a writer can make. Plagiarism is a crime. A person who steals another person's words can wind up in jail."

Another time during a class meeting, she said I couldn't be nominated for class favorite because I had been it last year. "Nice girls are not pigs," she said. "They don't hog all the attention for themselves."

"Miss Beasley, I didn't nominate myself!"

"That's enough, Cecil McRae. I am the sponsor of this class and I lead the meetings."

Sitting in study hall, I took the pictures and the letters out of my notebook. There were four pictures. One was obviously Cousin Irene smiling with a great tray of food in her arms. The three others were baby pictures, the kind that come inside a cardboard frame with two flaps closing over the front to keep the picture safe: a baby in a woman's arms, a baby in an old fashioned cap and dress, and a baby in a white sailor suit trying to salute.

I laid the pictures aside and began examining the letters. Not letters really, more like notes. Six small envelopes yellowed and brittle each addressed in pencil to Mrs. Rachel McRae, Windham, Mississippi. One from New Orleans, four from Chicago, and the last from Miami. Each envelope contained a single sheet of white paper folded once.

July 14, 1904
New Orleans

Dearest Rachel, This is the only letter I am allowed to write and it is to say I am fine. It's over. However, the nuns say I must stay four more weeks. Irene.

August 21, 1904
Chicago

Dearest Rachel, I finally made it. Mrs. Boussard is a very kind woman. She said she will write occasionally and send a picture whenever she can. Irene.

Christmas, 1904
Chicago

Dearest Rachel, Here is the picture of my darling. Please keep it safe. Irene.

September 10, 1905
Chicago

Dearest Rachel, Another picture at last. Isn't he a handsome baby. He has four teeth and is crawling. He had a bout of croup but nothing serious. They expect to go to Florida for Christmas. Her people are from there. Irene.

December 1, 1907
Chicago

Dearest Rachel, No word for two years. Now this, Mr. Boussard died last spring. Mrs. Boussard is returning to Florida to marry. The new husband will adopt the baby, but she is not to write again. Irene.

July 14, 1909
Miami

Dearest Rachel, I am lost.

"What are you up to now?" Miss Beasley demanded. "Cecil McRae, will you look at me, Young Lady? I do not allow note passing in study hall. School is no place for idle gossip spread by silly girls. Bring that trash to me, please. Right now!"

Sorrow and anger swelled my insides. I couldn't breathe. My eyes wouldn't blink. I was humiliated. I was lost.

"I don't care what you allow in study hall, Miss Beeswax. I don't care about you and I don't care about this school! I'm sorry for you."

I realized I was standing, clenched fist, shouting like no tomorrow. Suddenly, my knees buckled and I slipped to the floor.

Everyone was real quiet. Jerry Jenkins, the absolutely fattest boy in school and who claimed he was my boyfriend whispered, "You've done it this time, Cecil McRae. She's gone to get Mr. McCann."

I made it down to the girl's bathroom and started tearing up letters flushing them in the toilet. I tore pictures next. Dry cardboard, bits of faces, corners of a lace cap, a tiny little hand. All sucked down the drain. The back of the last picture read, "Merry Christmas—From our family to yours, Whitney Robert Boussard."

I wouldn't come out of the stall until Mama was there. I kept flushing and flushing. Not hearing one word Mr. McCann said.

Later at home, I told Mama I missed Grady and that I couldn't go back to school without him. I cried and cried, begging her to make him come home. Finally, she said we were going to State on Saturday. I could see Grady then.

The next Monday, I was back in school but not in Miss Beasley's class. I was in Miss Sinclair's room. She taught seniors, and her brother Mr. Sinclair was band director. She agreed to let me do eighth grade work if I could sit in the back and be quiet.

Why did I tear up the letters and the pictures? Was it to spite Miss Beasley or was it to hide what I knew from myself. I never told. I never told anyone what I knew. Not even Grady.

Doughnuts. I loved Shipley doughnuts, but I didn't go back to Mangum Ford ever again.

The Play

Wilma Cooper died last week. She was Mama's last surviving first cousin. Her father was Grandma Rachel's youngest brother Noel. Poor Wilma, married to J. J. Cooper and having all those children, her life was never easy.

Coopers go crazy. Old Mr. John Cooper, Wilma's father-in-law, lived fifteen years chained to a pole in his backyard. That was the best poor Miss Emma, Wilma's mother-in-law, could do. Mr. John wouldn't keep his clothes on, ranted night and day, and bit anyone getting close enough to catch. Miss Emma tethered him about twenty feet off the back porch. He had a little house just big enough for a bed and could reach the outhouse and the well. Mr. Newsom of the D'Leaux Trim and Barber Shop went out once a month. He saw to Mr. John's hygiene. Otherwise, Mr. John was better left alone.

One time after a really public episode with J. J, I asked, "Mama, why would any sensible woman marry a Cooper? What possessed Wilma to do such a thing?"

"Wilma married Jay Jay Cooper because she didn't want to be an old maid, Little Bit."

"Honestly, Mama, did she have to pick a Cooper?"

"It was the Depression, Cecil McRae. All the men who could leave had left looking for work. Most of them went to Mobile like Uncle Otis and Uncle Dewey. Some went farther. That's how Jerry and Priscilla Jane came to have family in Chicago. They have two Jenkins uncles and an aunt who went there for work and never came back.

"If I hadn't gone with your Grandpa John to Tennessee when Mr. McPherson died, I might have wound up with a Cooper. That's where I met your father, at Mr. McPherson's funeral.

"Wilma needed a husband. She saw an opportunity with John Jason Cooper and didn't hesitate. She snapped him up."

That's what Evelyn did. She didn't want to be an old maid. She saw an opportunity with Grady and didn't hesitate. She got Grady with me right there watching, unable to do a thing.

What's worse, Evelyn is my fault.

It happened my sophomore year at The W, The Mississippi University for Women in Columbus. Evelyn was the hall monitor on my dorm room floor. She never left campus, didn't have a boyfriend, and talked constantly about "Daddy."

Grady was finishing his second year of vet school at State. I fixed Evelyn up with Grady so she would drive me to Starkville.

My English class was reading *Lysistrata* by Aristophanes and I could get extra credit by seeing the play. The performance was in Jackson on a Friday night. Grady was all for going but had a late lab. If I could meet him at State, we would go from there.

Lysistrata: There are a lot of things about us women
That sadden me, considering how men
See us as rascals.
Calonice: As indeed we are!

We were deciding whose assessment of women was correct. Seeing the play was supposed to help.

Going to The W was opposite the Depression. Marriageable men were everywhere. Mississippi State was thirty-five miles away, and the only women at State were cows. Grady said that, not me. On weekends, State boys cruised the streets of Columbus honking horns, laughing, and generally being obnoxious—anything to get noticed while W girls strolled tree lined sidewalks being proper Southern ladies. W girls could not have cars until they were seniors. Evelyn was a senior.

When I told Evelyn that Grady needed a date for the weekend, but we had to meet him in Starkville, she didn't hesitate.

"Your brother? A date? Jackson? Of course I'll go.

"You are the sweetest sister, Cecil McRae, taking care of your brother. Men are lost without us. Aren't they."

I should have said then and there it wasn't a real date. Grady hadn't mentioned a date. I should have said, but I didn't.

"Is Grady in vet school or does he want to go to vet school?

"Did you say we are spending two nights in Jackson? I love the Robert E. Lee Hotel. Don't you? I've stayed there lots of times with Daddy."

Evelyn babbled on about Jackson and how much fun we were going to have.

Months later, when I finally considered why Evelyn never left Campus—why she didn't spend Saturdays trolling along picking up boys like pebbles on a beach—I knew the truth. Evelyn was a cow, a cow disguised as my hall monitor.

We drove to Starkville; met Grady and of course, Jerry Jenkins. Jerry tagged along with Grady everywhere he went. Jerry joined

Delta Tau Epsilon, the veterinary boys' fraternity, even though he was an accounting major.

By the time we left for Jackson, Evelyn had transformed. I couldn't believe it. My quiet, helpful hall monitor became a darling of the Delta. When Grady mentioned his animal husbandry lab, her giggle was like champagne bubbles. They overwhelmed her innocent, intoxicated brain.

"Oh, Grady," she confessed, "I love that you are a vet, but my daddy is a cotton farmer. We don't know about those things in the Delta."

Lysistrata turned out to be a really funny play.

After it was over, we walked down to Primo's for dessert. Primo's was my favorite place. In high school, we ate there every time the band went to Jackson for Contest. The restaurant had black and white tile floors, white tablecloths, and red leather chairs with brass tacks hammered in neat little lines all around the upholstery. Seated in the big round booth in the corner, we ordered the specialty of the house, cherry pie à la mode.

Then Jerry proposed.

He got out of the booth, went down on one knee and pledged again his unending love and implored me to accept his unworthy humble self. One word from me would make him the happiest man in the world. Only I could be the answer to his prayers.

Evelyn squealed, "How romantic! How absolutely divine!"

"For the millionth time, Jerry," I said. "No, I am not going to marry you."

Jerry Jenkins started proposing to me in eighth grade and I started saying "No." He never believed me.

Evelyn didn't believe me either.

"Cecil McRae," she protested, "That poor man is in agony. He loves you. You must say yes. How can you be so cruel!"

There he was on his knees holding up this huge ring. Not a diamond ring—costume jewelry, a big ball-looking thing covered in silver glitter. Jerry proposed every chance he got. It was a joke.

Suddenly, everyone in Primo's was watching. Evelyn was crying.

Finally I said, "Yes, Jerry, I am saying yes I will marry you. But you must promise never to ask me again."

He leaped from his knees, gave me a kiss, then bowed to the crowd.

In the middle of the applause, Jerry laughing and bowing, Evelyn made her move.

"Do I seem a fading flower?" she said. " Is chivalry really dead? Am I to be the only old maid at this table?"

What could Grady do? He got out of the booth, down on one knee and proposed. He even offered Evelyn Jerry's gaudy ring as testament to his undying devotion to her unfailing beauty.

It was a joke. A silly joke. Everyone knew that. I certainly did.

By the time we got back to Columbus Sunday night, Evelyn was discussing bridesmaids, wedding invitations and married student housing at State. "Daddy" came the next weekend to meet Grady, and Evelyn went to Windham for Easter. They married the day after Evelyn's graduation from The W.

Evelyn was Wilma Cooper made over: she saw an opportunity and didn't hesitate. She snapped Grady up.

And the ring, the engagement ring? It was a symbol of Grady's impetuous love. She told the story to anyone getting close enough to catch, "Grady, down on his knees in Primo's. Only his heart and this silly ring to offer. How could I refuse? Of course I said 'yes.' Saying 'no' would have been too cruel."

The Top Hat Club

Sandra Dale Peterson was a kleptomaniac. Maybe the only one I've ever known. Kleptomaniacs steal things. That's what Sandra did. She and I were in Psychology 101 together at The W and became friends. I fixed her up with Allen Sandrinos. She and her roommate Allison Yeager were both What Knots from Meridian and really popular.

Dr. Ratcliff called kleptomania the "rich ladies' " disease. He didn't think much of it. Neither did I until my new Weejuns disappeared and I spent that weekend with Sandra Peterson.

Sandra Dell was the first person I knew whose parents were divorced. She had a little sister who was ten and lived with her mother. Sandra lived with her dad. I couldn't believe their house. It looked like the inside of a fancy furniture store. Even the glasses matched. Sandra had everything. A king sized bed—I didn't know such things existed, her own television, a private bathroom just like in a hotel, and a telephone which wasn't an extension phone like in a kitchen, but her own personal number. Sandra hated everything about the place. It wasn't her real home. Her mother had the real house. The court gave it to her in the divorce. Sandra and her dad were just waiting for the alimony to run out. When it did, her mother and little sister would have to move.

The only reason Sandra ever went home was to buy makeup. Fine Brothers Madison mixed it especially for her. It was green. It didn't look green unless you held it up against something white. But it was definitely green. Sandra had blonde, blonde hair and a movie star complexion. When I looked at her, I thought of White Rain shampoo advertisements. One picture all slick and shiny would cover the entire back of a magazine. The girl in the picture was perfect and always blonde with marble white skin. Her head would be turned slightly to one side showing off her gorgeous Grace Kelly hair.

"You too can be a White Rain Girl," the magazine promised. Not me, I thought; but Sandra Peterson could.

It was the make up. When she washed the green off, her skin was all red and puffy. Seeing her like an over ripe tomato all red and swollen made me suspicious of those magazines. Without green makeup, Sandra didn't match her perfect house.

A phobia I could understand. Luther John Matthews had a phobia. Luther worked at the Purina feed store in D'Leaux and was afraid of water. Wouldn't go near it. He wouldn't even sit in a boat on dry land. Luther thought someone meant to drown him. He just didn't know who or when. Someone somewhere was going to wake up one morning and decide, "I'm going to drown Luther Matthews today;" then go do it.

Luther couldn't sell a bag of chicken feed without worrying about water. He had a certified phobia. But a maniac? A person having to do something over and over—washing his hands a thousand times a day, flipping light switches on and off, knocking three times on a door then three times again and again—seemed a bit unlikely. It was unlikely until I met Sandra Dale Peterson.

Luther looked crazy. Maybe that was part of the problem. Sandra Dell looked normal. More than normal. And she was from Meridian. Being from Meridian was not like being from Hot Water or Stringer. Meridian Mississippi, was a legitimately desirable hometown. It had a city park with a swimming pool, two hospitals, and restaurants instead of cafes. No one from Hot Water or Stringer was ever going to be a What Knot.

The What Knot Society was the best club on campus. Popular, pretty girls from places like Natchez, Jackson, or The Coast, were usually What Knots or Dot's Daughters. An ordinary girl from say Piney Stump or Tuckertown had to be a Modern Maid, a Twiddle-de-Wink, or a True Explorer. But in order to join a club, any girl, popular, pretty or not, had to first receive a formal invitation and then she had to pass initiation. Doing things correctly at The W was just as important as doing things right.

The week before initiation, club pledges did all sorts of stupid stuff. A What Knot pledge had to answer any question she was asked by saying, "What knot." Then she had to knock three times on her head and shout, "Nobody home. Go away!" You could ask her again, but she would never actually answer the question.

Dot's Daughters carried around adoption papers wailing about being orphans. "I'm all alone in the cruel, cruel world," a pledge would cry. "Oh, woe is me!" If a girl lost her papers or got them stolen, and that did happen, she remained an orphan forever. Dot wouldn't adopt her.

Sandra and I became friends on account of Allen Sandrinos. What Knots went into spasms at the mention of his name. Just about everybody did. Allen was the best-looking guy at Mississippi State and drove a lavender air-conditioned Chevrolet Impala. I knew all about him. He was in vet school and a friend of Grady's. He had been dating Jennifer Simpson, a Dot's Daughter, but she transferred to Ole Miss. With Jennifer gone, Allen was obviously available. I fixed him up with Sandra.

At The W, when something went missing, we didn't accuse people of stealing. We put a note on the bulletin board. We were ladies: proper, courteous young women. Occasionally we might borrow something and forget to return it. The note was supposed to remind whoever had borrowed the missing something to please bring it back. No hard feelings.

I wrote my polite note concerning the forgotten borrowed shoes, posted it among the many other polite notes, and left with Sandra for the Top Hat Club and a rendezvous with Allen Sandrinos. The Top Hat Club was just south of the Meridian city limits off the highway up a really steep hill. I didn't know it existed, but Meridian girls talked about it all the time. Guys from the naval air station went there. The music was great and girls got in free.

Within twenty minutes of walking in, Sandra was practicing her magic on Allen Sandrinos, and I was having the time of my life. James David Martin, a newly graduated-from-Annapolis naval officer was practicing magic on me. Within an hour, Sandra Dell had totally replaced Jennifer Simpson, and I was in love with Meridian.

Saturday morning, Sandra and I roamed around downtown. I thought we were having a nice day and felt really stupid after it was over. Sandra used a charge card for her make up, then shoplifted a belt and jacket from Fine Brothers, a purse from Marks Rothenburg, and a belt and another pair of shoes from Steppin' Out on the Town. I didn't even realize she had the stuff until we were back at her house. We were together the entire day and I never saw her take a thing.

She did it again Saturday night but not with shoes and purses. Allen couldn't meet us at the Top Hat Club so Sandra shoplifted my boyfriend.

"How could that happen Grady," I said. "I didn't see a thing. We're at the Top Hat Club. Everything's wonderful. Jimmy is laughing and dancing telling me about Annapolis. I turn my head and he's disappeared with my best friend."

"She snaked your date. Little Bit. It happens but it's not a crime."

"But Grady, Jimmy Martin was mine. She stole something that was mine and she knew what she was doing."

"Call it stealing if you like, Little Bit. But he wasn't kidnapped. He wanted to go or he wouldn't have left."

"It was stealing, Grady. And, she took my shoes. They were in her dorm room still in the box. What am I supposed to tell Allen? That his new girlfriend looks like a beauty queen but is actually a kleptomaniac and a thief wearing magic makeup?"

"Allen isn't what he looks like either," Grady replied. "Not exactly."

"Not exactly what? Grady. Not handsome, and rich, and in vet school?"

"His name isn't even Allen, Little Bit. It's Alejandro. He wants to be Allen because it sounds more American. And he's definitely not rich. He just looks rich. His father came from Cuba and runs a dry cleaners in Miami."

"But he is in vet school, Isn't he? He can't be lying about that too, Grady. Can he?"

"Allen's grades are so low, he's trying to repeat the entire first year. He can't see it yet, but Allen's washed out."

"It's not fair, Grady," I complained.

"What's not fair? That Allen can't pass Introduction to Bovine Anatomy? He hasn't passed because he hasn't studied."

"It's not fair because Allen's not real. He's a phony. But girls practically faint when he walks through a room. Sandra has enough stuff crammed under her bed to open a clothing store. No one says a word. She's still popular. I don't care how many polite notes we put on that bulletin board, she isn't remembering to give anything back."

"People see what they want to see, Cecil McRae. We choose what is real and not real."

"Do you really believe that Grady? We see something and must decide whether or not it's real? We decide reality for ourselves?"

"That might be right," Grady said. "I've been looking at things especially this year trying to decide just that: what things are real."

"What did you decide? Grady, Is Sandra Dell Peterson real?"

"Sandra Dale Peterson is your decision, Little Bit. I have decided cows are real. Cows are on my list. They are definitely real."

"Cows?"

"Cows, Little Bit."

"Why, Grady? Why are you so sure about cows?"

"I can trust a cow to be a cow. A cow can only be a cow, nothing else. And consider this, Cecil McRae, I have never known one to steal a pair of shoes."

The Chicken Salad

The D'Leaux Women's Auxiliary held their annual officer's luncheon today and I went. Evelyn is the in-coming president and I was her special guest. I made a mess of Evelyn's meeting. And I'm sorry.

The Auxiliary grew out of Mama's ladies' club. Originally, ten friends met once a month in each others' homes. It was mostly country women living with a parent or two on old home places. The women would meet in the evening to visit and discuss community concerns. Now it's fifty women meeting for lunch at the D'Leaux Inn and Restaurant. The members plan things for people they don't even know, and Auxiliary members aren't necessarily even friends. Membership is by invitation only.

Evelyn can't say enough about The Auxiliary: eye screening for all first graders, the puppet show about healthy teeth, free toothbrushes.

"Cecil McRae," she said, "you'd be surprised by the number of people in Mounds County who have never heard of flossing."

I tried to like The Auxiliary, but just couldn't do it. What's the sense in paying fifty dollars to join a club and then having to pay two dollars if you miss a meeting? Maybe I have something to do at twelve o'clock the second Tuesday of the month, and I shouldn't be charged two dollars for doing it.

The Auxiliary now has a yearbook and everyone's name and responsibilities are listed. Each member must be on two committees and serve as leader for at least one project or host a meeting. Members can request committee assignments, which will be honored if possible. However, the president with her advisory council decides all committee assignments. Their decision is final.

Evelyn loves deciding.

Things weren't always so strict. The ladies' club was actually lots of fun. I remember one time when Mama was hostess, Rose, Grady, and I served the refreshments. While the meeting was going on, Grady and I fixed the plates.

"Grady," Mama said, "put one lettuce leaf onto each snack plate. Make sure it's dry first. The ice cream scoop of chicken salad goes on top of the leaf. Little Bit, you can put on the spiced peach and three Ritz crackers. But be neat. This is for ladies and ladies like things extra neat."

Rose's job was to fix the glasses and serve the tea.

One really good thing about that meeting was the screens. Samson McDougle, Bigman's brother, had helped Uncle Dewey; and all the windows, doors and both porches were now completely covered in new silvery metal screens. Mama dragged the big kitchen table onto the back porch and dressed it up like Sunday. With the dark outside and no flies or mosquitoes, the porch floated in a bubble of light, a fancy little room; and we were fancy folks.

Following the meeting which was really just a reading of the minutes, a discussion of who was sick or needed help, and the birthday party for the State School, Miss Rhinehart who was president would adjourn. Rose was to come into the living room and say, "Would you ladies care for some refreshment on the porch?"

When the ladies were settled, Rose was to pour the tea starting with Miss Rhinehart. That was Grady's and my signal to bring in the plates.

We did it just right. Rose said her part. And the ladies noticed the screens and mentioned how lucky Mama was to have Uncle Dewey to help out.

When Rose served the tea, it was the way things happen in dress-up restaurants, all smiling and gracious. "Would you care for tea Miss Rhinehart?" Rose asked. "Yes Ma'am, it's sweet." Then she continued on around the table ending with Mama.

Grady took Miss Rhinehart her plate, and then like the shoemaker's elves we finished the job. Everyone had their plate lickey-d-split. Mama gave a big compliment to Rose for serving the tea and to Grady and me for fixing the plates. Then we excused ourselves inside to hear the radio. Turned way down with no fussing.

On Tuesdays Rose always wanted *Fibber McGee and Molly* on WKAY in Birmingham. Grady wanted WWL in New Orleans and *Gunsmoke.* I don't remember who won, but we were quiet. The ladies' club was Mama's treat and we wanted her to have it.

All these years later, I wanted Evelyn to have her treat as well. I wanted her first meeting as President of The D'Leaux Women's Auxiliary to be perfect. Honestly, I did.

It had rained really hard last night, but the day started off clear and fine. I had my clothes laid out; my purse, my shoes, a handkerchief, and car keys were ready. Then I remembered: today is the second Tuesday of March; it's turnip day.

Wanda Strickland is my nearest neighbor and the kindest woman on earth. She does something good for someone every single day. By the end of March, turnip roots get pithy and the leaves are tough. Before that happens, Wanda clears her row and takes everyone a nice big mess of roots and tops. She especially remembers those too old or sick to manage a garden. It's lots of work to pull, bundle, and tie an entire row of turnips, and Wanda's well over seventy. I ran over and helped as long as I could, then hurried home, jerked on my dress, grabbed my purse and was out the door lickey-d-split.

The banquet room at the D'Leaux Inn and Restaurant is through the motel lobby all the way to the back of the building. It was a rush but I was at the luncheon by twelve.

The decorating committee had gone all out with a South Seas motif. A grass skirted hostess "Aloha-ed" me at the sign-in table and put a crepe paper lei around my neck. Another hostess served me pineapple juice in a punch cup sporting a tiny umbrella. A huge painted sunset hung across the wall nearest the kitchen, and the buffet bar had transformed into a tiki hut complete with thatched roof and bamboo stools. Cloth printed with palm trees and parrots covered the tables and hula-girl bobble heads bobbled away as centerpieces. Bringing Bali Hai to D'Leaux was a lot of work but everyone seemed pleased with the effect. Fancy folks indeed.

"If you ladies would finish your visiting and take a seat, refreshments will now be served."

Evelyn's first presidential decision.

When Birdie Johnson, a *Gidget Goes Hawaiian* look alike set my plate down, I thought back to that evening on the porch, the cloth on the table, the screens, Rose serving tea. And Grady and me racing back and forth seeing who could reach the plates first. Grady was kind of fat and the sleeve of his plaid shirt was torn. He snagged it on the fence that afternoon trying to beat me home. Grady was the biggest but I was the fastest. I thought about Mama's compliment.

"Grady and Cecil McRae made up the plates for us this evening and have done such a sweet job of serving. Thank you, Grady. Thank you, Cecil McRae. Now be excused quietly while we visit."

What a mess we had made and how long it took me to remember.

Mama's chicken salad was too dry and crumbly so we doctored it up with mayonnaise. Then Grady decided such a tiny taste of chicken salad wouldn't satisfy a gnat. We used china plates instead of the snack set and Grady filled a coffee cup twice full of chicken salad for each lettuce leaf. Those leaves didn't stand a chance. They were completely smothered under a white avalanche of greasy goo. We put on not one but three spiced peaches and a generous helping of Grandma Rachel's bread and butter pickles along with a healthy chunk of red hoop cheese. We finished off our improvements by dividing the entire box of crackers among the ten plates.

Like Grady said, "Who eats just three Ritz crackers anyway?

Looking at my dainty little plate and surrounded by The Auxiliary's idea of tropical paradise, I had to agree with Grady. Such a tiny taste of chicken salad wouldn't satisfy a gnat.

I couldn't help but laugh. Then I cried. Something about everything seemed really sad.

At home later the phone rang. I didn't want to answer, but I did.

"Yes, Evelyn, you have every right to be mad and I apologize. I'm sorry I cried and I'm sorry about the mess. I am really sorry.

"Yes, I agree entirely. Tracking mud through your meeting in a pair of old garden boots does seem disrespectful of you and your presidency.

"No, I am not jealous, Evelyn. I am absolutely not jealous of you or your presidency. It was turnip day at Wanda's.

I just forgot to change my shoes."

The Grief Process

"Maude's Standard Florist was a beacon of truth in the flower world. We do not over speak to say a Maude Standard arrangement could be spotted across a graveyard as easily as across a funeral parlor. Oh, Dear Maude, how greatly you are missed."

—*Mounds Monitor*— Edwin Minor reporting

Maude Standard Dunn's obituary did not over speak. Even though she has been gone nearly a year, her funeral arrangements remain a floral benchmark for the county; and her husband Lloyd still cries in church every Sunday. Now Tyler, Maude's youngest son, is home declaring her body isn't buried. He's come all the way from California to put her into the ground himself. Oh, Dear Maude, how greatly you are missed.

Lloyd Dunn was Maude's second husband. Stanford Standard, Maude's first husband, died in Vietnam. The Vietcong blew him up. Nothing was left, not even his dog tags. Maude used his death benefit to buy a storefront on Court Street and raised her babies Buddy and Tyler right there in the shop. She was a widow for years before she married Lloyd. The romance actually began over the coffin arrangement for Lloyd's first wife Bernice.

"My heart went out to Lloyd," Maude said. "If a man exists that can love a woman, that man is Lloyd Dunn."

Maude taught him flower arranging and ordered urns and pots for Bernice's grave. One arrangement led to another and love bloomed.

Buddy, Maude's oldest boy, was a natural athlete. As a child, his picture was in the paper every week shaking hands with some official or accepting some big award. He was the fastest, strongest, most talented student ever to play sports for D'Leaux. His senior year, college recruiters swarmed around him like flies. But it wouldn't do. The day he finished high school, Buddy signed up for the Marines.

"He joined the Marines to be with his dad," Grady said. "Sergeant Standard was a hero and Buddy was following him onto the field of battle."

He didn't get there. Buddy died in Alaska. A car accident. He hit a moose. The problem was Buddy's remains. According to his enlistment papers if death occurred while on active duty, PFC Buddy Standard requested to be buried where he fell. Alaska is not Southeast Asia, but final requests are final requests. The Marines buried Buddy in a military cemetery at Juno, Alaska.

"I let Stanford go," Maude cried. "It was war. He's in pieces somewhere in a jungle, scattered around like confetti. But the government shouldn't do this to me again. I want Buddy, not another death benefit."

Maude didn't get Buddy. But she did eventually accept the flag and the money. Lloyd helped her. He did it with flowers.

The Dunns originally settled in western Mounds. Dunn's Hill is the highest point in the county. Most of the Dunns sold out to Georgia Pacific in the 1950's, but the few that are left respect the family burial plot. When Bernice died, Chester Ray, Lloyd's son, took over the used car business and Lloyd started improving the cemetery.

"Cecil McRae, that cemetery saved Lloyd's life. Then it saved mine," Maude said. "I'd sold flowers for years, but had never planted one. Lloyd talked me into it. I planted a memorial for Buddy. I came back to life down on my knees holding a gladiola bulb. That's how I want to be remembered, covered with glads."

The Dunn cemetery is what got Tyler upset. *Mississippi Magazine* featured it in an article on family cemeteries and private burial sites.

Tyler Standard is the exact opposite of his brother Buddy. Tyler wouldn't follow anyone anywhere unless it involved sequins. He's a hairdresser in Los Angeles. "Stylist to the Stars," he calls himself. Pictures of Tyler doing things to famous people hung all around Maude's shop. He flew to Santa Barbara once to do Oprah Winfrey's eyebrows.

"Oprah's secretary called me," Tyler said. "I thought it was Karl playing a joke, but it wasn't. Really Karl shouldn't have been so upset for me not believing what he said. Who expects a call from Oprah Winfrey's secretary?"

Tyler's roommate Karl is from Minnesota and works for Disney. He was going into pictures but got sidetracked into marketing. Karl always sent Maude fabulous birthday presents and something even better for Christmas even though he's Jewish.

Oprah Winfrey's private jet flew Tyler to Santa Barbara.

Maude told everyone she saw for months and months about Tyler and the eyebrows.

I feel connected to Oprah. The entire world feels connected to Oprah, but I think I really am. I think I know Oprah, and that Oprah knows me. On some level, in the deepest, most cellular well of consciousness, Cecil MeRae Britton and Oprah Winfrey are friends. That could be right. We were in Kosciusko at the same time. She lived out from Kosciusko, and I stayed there two weeks when I was twelve. I went with Priscilla Jane Jenkins to visit her aunt. She was Prissy Jane then. Mama made me go. Priscilla Jane's Aunt Alice wasn't married and didn't have children. She said we were gal pals and had to stick together. Aunt Alice smoked and had a boyfriend she didn't really like.

"Men are good for some things," she said. "But precious few."

We went to the First Baptist Church Bible School and learned about Paul. The night before we left, Kenny Adams kissed Pricilla Jane on Aunt Alice's front porch. Oprah was in Kosciusko all that time and I didn't know it.

Tyler didn't get a picture of Oprah like he wanted; but he did get a picture of her hand throwing chicken feed. Tyler was from Mississippi; so after the eyebrows, Oprah took him out to see her chickens and gather eggs. He left with six Bantam chicken eggs and one blurry shot of Oprah Winfrey's fingers. He and Karl blew out the eggs and saved the shells. Maude got one of the empty eggs for Mother's Day.

When Maude died, Tyler was on location with a survivor reality show and couldn't get home for the funeral. He roared into D'Leaux last week with a copy of *Mississippi Magazine* angry as hops with poor Lloyd.

It was the cemetery.

"According to the article," Tyler said reading from the magazine,

" ' ...the cemetery sits on the eastern edge of Dunn's Hill up a winding gravel road overhung with live oaks and Spanish moss. Meandering pathways lead the visitor past ancestral graves, memorial columns, and amazing statuary, all surrounded by carefully tended beds of blooming flowers.' "

"I'm not surprised by how well maintained things are," I said. "Lloyd's out there working most everyday."

"It gets better, Cecil McRae, much better," Tyler continued. " 'The centerpiece of this eulogy to death is a silent procession of classic cars. The solemn cortege is lead by a vintage Packard hearse transporting a pale yellow coffin topped with white gladiolas. Mr. Dunn assembled *Entering the Dreaming City* as a tribute to his late wife Maude Standard Dunn.' "

"Mother's coffin was yellow and she had an arrangement of white glads. I have pictures," Tyler said. "She's not buried, Cecil McRae. My mother is lying in the back of a rusted out Packard and reporters are gawking at her through the windows."

Grady thinks Tyler has PTSD, Post Traumatic Stress Disorder.

"Dogs get it," Grady said. "I see it after every hunting season, and Tyler's a lot more sensitive than a dog. His father, his brother, then his mother, all died. Tyler didn't experience their deaths. He wasn't there. Tyler needs to process his loss."

Lloyd was in church this morning. Not crying.

"How are you today, Lloyd?" I asked.

"Better," he said. "I'm doing better. I had help yesterday with my mulching. I had a real good day."

"Did Tyler help?"

"Tyler? No, no, not Tyler. He's gone. Doris Henderson came out. One of her cousins married Oriss Dunn. They didn't have children. She's sprucing up their graves. She has time now with Pat gone; the evenings get awfully lonesome she said. We worked together all afternoon."

"Where's Tyler?"

"Gone back to California," Lloyd said. "A friend of his read the cemetery article and really liked it. Tyler had Doris take a picture of him and me in front of the Packard then he was off like a man on fire. Couldn't leave fast enough. Something to do with eyebrows."

The Orange Poppies

The print of orange poppies hanging in the dining room was art. I didn't know that growing up. I realized the truth about those poppies standing in the Museum of Art in New Orleans my sophomore year at Columbus.

Grandma Rachel didn't have the concept of unuseful things. Objects serving no purpose in and of themselves. She drew no comfort from ornament unnecessary for life. Her house, which had been her mother's house and her grandmother's before that, was a place of utility. Layers and layers of time and use but no record of frivolity. Memories were not displayed on tables, nor emotions hung on walls. Maybe one picture, like a wedding portrait might be there. But that was an event stopped in time. The people in the captured scene existed only as confirmation of that past reality.

Standing in the New Orleans Museum of Art, an entire building filled only with unuseful and unnecessary things, I wondered why such things came to exist? Who thought them necessary? Without being aware, tears began slipping down my cheeks dropping from my chin.

"Mama," I asked later, "Why are those poppies in the dining room? Where did they come from?

"Uncle Dewey bought that table and chairs when he got a job at the paper mill in Mobile, she said. "He was so proud of himself. The picture came with the set."

The Feed Store

Randal McMichael was in town the other day. Grady saw him going into Wyatt's feed store. He was wearing women's clothes and had sewn his lips together with a huge purple button tacked with red thread. I wasn't surprised by the dress or the button. The first time I saw Randal, he was wearing a dress out behind his grandpa's house. Chambliss Willard, Mama's first cousin, was Agnes Sommes' second husband. That's how we're connected.

Agnes's first husband was a McMichael from somewhere up in Michigan. She met him while going to school in New Orleans. This McMichael man took Agnes up North to be with his people and she lived there until he died. I never heard how he died, but Agnes came home a widow with twin boys Aaron and Michael, and a third boy Randal.

Cousin Chambliss married Agnes within a year.

The Sommes place is on the river just south of Big Pine. For generations the family farmed a huge rise still called Sommes Level. Once she married Chambliss and had JT, Agnes never left the place, but her daddy still got around pretty well. He came to town every now and then and would stop by to visit Grandma Rachel on the porch. Uncle Dewey wanted to say he was trying to court, but Grandma didn't take a tease about Rudolph Sommes. The Sommeses were Catholics descended from French fur traders who intermarried with the Indians long before the English arrived. Mr. Rudolph was a decent man whose sorrow was not his own making. Even so, being Catholic and having Indian blood were not fashionable in Mounds County.

The twins' drowning is my first real recollection of Randal. I must have been about six. I went with Mama and Grandma Rachel when they carried two lemon pies down to the house for after the funeral. The Sommes place sits at the end of a long narrow road that did wind through huge fields of cotton and corn, but no one has worked The Level for years. Everything now is wild and overgrown.

Mama and Grandma went inside to sit and sent me out to play with Randal. I found him wearing a dress beating on a bush with a stick. Branches of sweetshrub quivered and scented buds fell to earth with every stroke.

He was whispering, "I like you Miss Taylor, but you are a bad, bad girl!" When he saw me he stopped.

"I'm Cecil McRae Britton," I said. "Your new daddy is my Mama's cousin."

Honestly, I didn't think a thing about the dress. We were soon talking and laughing like friends. He had a blind hen he let me feed; then we climbed the mulberry tree in the chicken yard and ate mulberries until our fingers and mouths were purple.

After a bit Randal said, "You want to see something in the barn? It's a secret." Then he headed off toward the lot.

I followed him down the path past the garden and the outhouse to a wagon road marking the boundary between the main yard and the woods beyond. Just ahead was the cow lot and then a corn crib. Bantam chicks were scratching around the feed trough and a pig was off somewhere squealing. The barn sat just beyond the crib overshadowing the smaller structure like a fairytale giant might over stand a dollhouse. To my thinking, it was the biggest building I had ever seen. The two logged bins were actually huge raised rooms facing each other about ten feet apart with stalls built on the outside ends. A tin roof still shiny and slick covered the entire structure. I thought we were going to climb up and slide, but Randal hurried on under the overhanging tin and into the wide run separating the bins. He stopped and waited listening like a dog, his head cocked to one side. Down on all fours, he went under a bin motioning me to follow. I squatted down under the bin crouching as low as I could. Waddling along like a duck, I followed Randal who was creeping away toward one of the stalls.

In the twilight under the bin, everything was hot and still. the air heavy with the smell of dead rats. I could hear the buzz of flies and around my feet the dirt lay dry and dimpled. I crept on catching up with Randal who was now squatted peering into the stall beyond. White light shining through gaps between the planks struck like a knife jabbing my head. I stopped a second blinking into the brightness.

Randal's dusty hand covered my mouth as he guided my eyes toward the light and what I came to see. Being taller by a head, I had to bend down, my shoulders brushing my knees.

There was Chambliss holding a hammer beside a mound of dirty sacks covered with flies. Flies, thousands and thousands of angry flies swarmed around the stall like bees on robbing day. Heat and stench pushed through the cracks like air escaping a fire. Chambliss didn't seem to notice. Bits of new lumber and sawdust lay around his work boots.

I wet my pants. Randal held fast to my mouth. Hot liquid running down my legs onto my feet.

The boxes were finished. They rested on a plank table ready to be filled. Against the wall, two lids waited for their nails.

Wrenching Randal's hand away, I mouthed, "Let's go. Let's go!"

Randal didn't move. His eyes magnets drawn to the light.

I crawled back toward the run. Once clear of the bin, I ran and ran. A hammer beating my chest taking my breath.

Randal found me at the pump. "You didn't see. Stupid! You wouldn't even look! I take you down there and you chickened out. What makes you so stupid!"

I didn't want to look. My eyes followed the water as it slid the dirt and pee down my bare legs and away into the uncut grass. I pumped and pumped the water stronger and stronger, an ice cold gushing flood.

For the longest time, I forgot that day and what Randal said I didn't see. I didn't even remember Chambliss whistling until just now.

The Beauty Pageant

Savannah Strengthford spent most of last Saturday hysteri-cal. The Our Pre-teen Queen pageant was scheduled for that Saturday night and Savannah was trying out for sixth grade queen. She was afraid the pageant would be cancelled. If that happened she wouldn't get to wear her dress.

Everyone connected to the pageant was hysterical. Dee Dee Dobbs who sponsored the event didn't show up for the picture session that afternoon and wasn't answering her phone. She and her husband Tommy had left the afternoon before taking Arlo Burney to Wiedman's in Meridian for supper. Apparently they had not returned. Arlo was Dee Dee's beauty mentor and head judge for the pageant.

J.J. Cooper was hysterical too. But not about the pageant. It was his cats. They disappeared. First it was Tabby Toes, then Blazer, now Blind Kitty Sam. Coopers, especially the men, go crazy. Mostly harmless but crazy. J.J. eats only three bean salad out of a can with a plastic spoon. Everything else is poison. And, he collects cats.

J.J. was married to mother's cousin Wilma who died last

summer. He hasn't worn a stitch of clothes since the funeral, which he didn't attend, and spends his days roaming the woods picking up feral cats. The sick ones he brings to Grady. The others get Meow Mix at feeding stations he's built along the river. The missing cats have had him upset for weeks.

"I know what's happening to my cats, Cecil McRae," he said Saturday morning.

"It's aliens. Aliens are stealing my cats. I'm shooting the thieving bastards."

"If illegal aliens are taking your cats, J.J, let the government handle it. Shooting homeless Mexicans is against the law."

"Not illegal aliens, Cecil McRae. Alien aliens. Creatures from outer space. I've found their base in the river at Sommes Landing. I'm going to get Tabby Toes back and give those cat-stealing sons of bitches a one way ticket back to Mars."

The beauty pageant went on despite the missing Dee Dee; Savannah wore her new dress; and Grady convinced J.J. to wait about the cats until the sheriff had time to investigate.

The aliens also had to wait. The Dobbs needed finding first. Tommy Dobbs was the football coach at D'Leaux High School. When he didn't show up at school Monday morning, Dee Dee's sister came down from Madison and filed a missing person's report.

Dee Dee Dobbs owns the Cheer Dance Win studio and runs it out of the old Piggly Wiggly building on Azalea Boulevard. She's painted "Winning is the Game" all over the building inside and out, and her students wear Winning-is-the-Game jackets to all their competitions.

By Monday afternoon, Find-Dee-Dee posters were all over town. So many people volunteered to help, Sheriff Turner set up a command center at the D'Leaux Inn and put Terry Clark, his deputy, to directing traffic. Tommy Dobbs coaches football. People like him just fine. But Dee Dee Dobbs can win. Everybody loves Dee Dee.

When the Dobbs came to D'Leaux five years ago, Dee Dee opened her Cheer Dance Win studio and started the Our Preteen Queen pageant. Dee Dee preaches winning. Winning is the game. Winning builds self-confidence and poise. She sponsors the pageant so all girls not just those in her classes can win.

For twenty-five dollars each contestant receives a one-hour lesson in stage presence, two tickets to the pageant, and an "I am a winner" tee shirt to wear at rehearsal. General admission costs five dollars and tee shirts for parents and friends sell for ten. Every year is a new color and every year is a sell out crowd.

By Tuesday afternoon, the D'Leaux Inn was a rainbow of "I am a winner" tee shirts. Sandra Freeman, Dee Dee's sister, organized a prayer vigil for Wednesday night and the whole town turned out. Despite the February weather, lots and lots of girls wore their pageant dresses.

Sandra, Dee Dee's sister, owns a used formal and bridal shop in Madison. She had sold most of the dresses on parade at the vigil. Every year before the pageant, she fills one end of the Piggly Wiggly with van loads of merchandise from her shop. Sandra's dresses are really nice and cost half the price of those at the Silver Slipper in Moss. When she comes to town, girls line up to buy pageant dresses, prom dresses, bridal dresses, anything they might need for the following year.

Sandra spoke at the vigil as did Robert Boswell, Arlo Burney's partner. He and Arlo are pageant professionals. They opened The

Queens Academy twenty years ago and have since trained hundreds of girls in pageant performance.

If Mississippi has beauty royalty, it's Burney and Boswell. They conduct pageant camps out of their antebellum home in Natchez. B and B as they are called turn awkward ducklings into graceful swans. Most girls attend two-week sessions, but a promising beauty may spend an entire year at the mansion preparing for a single event. Pictures of queens cover their walls and one room is dedicated exclusively to the B and B Miss Americas.

Sandra and Dee Dee are both alums of the school. According to Arlo, both sisters are true beauties but Dee Dee is a queen. Everyone in town would agree. Dee Dee Dobbs is the queen of D'Leaux.

After the prayer vigil Robert Boswell returned to Natchez and the academy's fledgling beauties. Sandra was able to stay until the weekend. Then she too had to leave.

The problem with the disappearance was the disappearance itself. Nothing else happened.

Tommy, Dee Dee, and Arlo were last seen Friday evening heading north out of town. They did not go to Wiedman's and did not have reservations as previously thought. The last charge on their credit card was for a tank of gas in Moss the week before and no withdrawals were made or checks written on their account after Thursday.

The highway patrol received no report involving a white Suburban on Mississippi roads, and no white Suburban was found abandoned anywhere.

After two weeks of false rumor and no leads, Cheer, Dance, Win closed; the vigil candles burned out; the rotted flowers carried to the dump; and Sheriff Dobbs, J J, and Grady headed for Sommes Level, Tabby Toes, and underwater alien bases.

The Mounds Monitor published the police report and the obituaries in the same issue: "Thomas Dobbs, Delores Dobbs, and Arlo Burney were found dead late Saturday afternoon in a car registered to Delores Dobbs. The automobile, a white Suburban, had rolled down a steep hill into the river below Sommes Landing. J.J. Cooper discovered the vehicle settled on the bottom in ten feet of water and notified authorities. The ignition was on, the windows were raised, and the doors locked. The victims suffered carbon monoxide poisoning and were dead before the accident occurred. No foul play was indicated."

Mr. Singley who owned the Piggly Wiggly building painted the whole thing white inside and out. Edward Massey took over as football coach; and J.J. Cooper started wearing clothes.

"Grady, do you know what's going on with J.J.?" I asked. "He was wearing an orange leisure suit this morning zipped all the way up to his Adam's apple."

"He wants to die with his clothes on, Little Bit."

"J.J. Cooper hasn't worn clothes willingly for years. What's happened to change his mind? Is J.J. dying?"

"The story will be out soon enough. You may as well hear it from me," Grady said. "But I hesitate to tell it."

"Hesitate to tell what?"

"It's the accident, Little Bit. The sight would make anyone wear clothes, even J.J. Dee Dee was in the front seat fully dressed slumped over a book. Arlo and Tommy were together in the back naked."

"Naked, Grady. Did you say Arlo and Tommy were naked?"

"Naked as birds, Cecil McRae. Even after two weeks on a muddy river bottom, what they were doing was perfectly clear. Dee Dee Dobbs may have been a true beauty," Grady said, "but Tommy Dobbs was the queen."

Miss Toufet

I had a surprise visitor today, Miss Imogene Toufet. Miss Toufet is a college student from North Carolina and was researching her family. She thought she might have a connection with Mounds County and wanted to know what she might find and where to look. She got pointed my way on account of Lottie Mae. Lottie Mae Toufet lived her entire life near Grandma Rachel and was my first friend. Miss Toufet comes through Lottie Mae's half brother Robert. He and his brother James left after their daddy died, and I didn't hear anything of them until Miss Toufet showed up all these years later wanting to know truth from fiction. How did her family stories match with mine. I was glad to tell her what I knew.

When Alexander Toufet came to Mounds in 1891, he was a widower with two young sons. He took possession of a two hundred acre farm ten miles south of Big Pine right where the railroad crosses the river going to Mobile. The old Wilkins place. Three years earlier, Brady Wilkins had pulled up stakes and gone to Texas. In those days, folks could see GTT nailed on houses and gate posts throughout the South. A universal farewell statement. If a man couldn't pay his taxes or owed more than he could ever hope to pay, GTT offered a way out. No guilt, no shame, just Gone To Texas.

Mr. Toufet paid the back taxes for those three years plus whatever else was owed on the property, and the land was his.

If colored folks were on a place when it changed hands, they stayed put. That was the case when Mr. Toufet moved with his two young sons onto the Wilkins home place. Ten or so Negro families, freed slaves or their children, lived in shacks around the fields scratching out an existence. After the war, thousands of their sisters and brothers flocked north. Many more stayed. Where do the old and infirm of spirit go?

Mr. Toufet began growing rice and by all accounts was a decent, hard working man. But it wouldn't do. Alexander Toufet wouldn't do. A well-educated, French-speaking man of color might own property and do business in New Orleans, but not in Mounds County, Mississippi. In the piney woods of Mississippi such a man did not exist. Light skinned, dark skinned, educated or not, Alexander Toufet was a Negro. A Negro full of ready money and grand ideas, but one who upset the nature of things in Mounds.

He married Corrine McDougle in 1896. By then he had expanded his original purchase from two hundred acres to five hundred, established a pay scale for his workers—a day's pay for a day's labor, and had opened a school for his tenants' children. A Catholic priest came from New Orleans to perform the ceremony; and as a wedding present, Alex Toufet gave his bride a brand new buggy complete with red padded leather seats and a brass handled buggy whip.

By 1904, he was becoming a powerful man. He owned over two thousand acres of land, had established a growing settlement with a cotton gin and a sawmill, and had even secured a stop on the GM&O railroad at what was now called Toufet Crossing.

The end came when he bought the Sanderson place. The Sandersons had settled in Mounds before 1810 and were one of the six families listed on the charter for Windham Presbyterian Church. Isaac Sanderson, his wife, and five children had reached Mississippi by crossing the Indian wilderness of Alabama rolling their household goods before them in barrels.

Thomas Boykin Sanderson, a man of limited ambition and skill but through no real fault of his own, was losing the last two hundred acres of that original homestead. Fine bottom land cleared and farmed by Sandersons for nearly a hundred years. Tom Boy hadn't paid his taxes in three years and owed more than he could ever hope to pay.

That afternoon a small crowd gathered near the courthouse steps to watch the proceedings. Some whispers may have reached Mr. Toufet's ears, but the drama unfolded without comment or obvious emotion. The Mounds Sentinel reported that of the twenty-seven parcels of land offered for sale, four were redeemed before the twelve o'clock deadline. Each of the twenty-three remaining parcels was sold to the highest bidder.

Mr. Toufet bid on three properties, got all three, and paid the Chancery Court clerk cash on what was owed.

For the Sanderson parcel, he outbid LeRoy Simms and John Cooper. After the clerk had receipted the cash and transferred the title, Mr. Toufet rode out to the Sanderson place to discuss whatever plans Tom Boy had for vacating the property. Realizing he had no such plans, Alex Toufet offered to keep Tom Boy on as a tenant or perhaps lease the property back provided both parties could reach an agreement as to terms. Mr. Toufet was conducting business, making what he thought a reasonable offer. To Thomas Boykin Sanderson it wasn't business nor was it a reasonable offer. It was an assault. A cowardly assault of the blackest kind.

The August night was hot, dry and noisy. The dog days of summer had not yet brought the expected downpour, and everywhere night creatures complained. Vast armies of frogs lay hidden in the darkness chanting, "rain, rain, rain," while everything from crickets to owls to wolves threatened riot with their screams.

The meeting place was the Indian mounds just south of Windham. First one rider, then another approached the burial ground tethering their horses just beyond the clearing in the edge of Cherokee Wood. Legend held that the site hosted the last Indian massacre in the state, The Battle of Mounds. Andrew Jackson was the hero of record, and the county's name commemorated the place.

Fifteen men waited shuffling back and forth checking their equipment much like soldiers for that first battle might have done: harnesses, guns, torches, ropes. All in order. Ben and Hugh Willard arrived late without their intended companion. They had thought to bring John McRae, their recently acquired brother-in-law, to the festivities but their invitation was refused. John McRae stayed home that night minding his wife Rachel.

The Defenders of Mounds, as the group called themselves, forded the river near Double Branches, and lighting their torches, charged the Wilkins place. They dragged Alexander Toufet from his house and shot him in the head. The house, the barn, the school, the fields, and finally the woods all burned that night. Only Mr. Toufet remained, hanging from a tree, dead pigs at his feet.

Corrine and the children made their way on foot in the dark to Grandma Rachel's corn crib. She found them the next morning mute with fear and exhaustion. At first she just kept them fed, warm and hidden. Later when the weather turned too cold for the barn, she quietly installed the family in Uncle Julian Horn's little house. Edward Dickens had built the house for his brother-in-law when his own family turned him out. Uncle Julian was a Civil War veteran and had cancer of the mouth. His face gradually dissolved into a mass of suffering and stench. Grandma remembered as a little girl standing by an open grave on a bitter cold day, a strong, big hand holding tightly to hers. Some brotherhood of the South erected a monument to him just inside the cemetery gates. The tall marble slab celebrated fallen heroes. It shattered years ago, but the small cast iron cross inscribed C S A still marks his place.

Alex Toufet's boys, James and Robert, ran off the next spring. But Corrine and the baby Lottie Mae stayed. Corrine died before I was born, but I remember Lottie Mae. She died churning butter on the back porch. I must have been five or six at the time.

Some good did come of that night's work. Alexander Toufet had died, but he became the last Negro man lynched in Mounds County. The self-proclaimed Defenders of Mounds were charged with murder not congratulated for valor. They were tried in a court of law, found guilty by a jury of their peers, and sent to prison. Ten white men went to Parchman for the murder of a Negro, a first for the state of Mississippi.

LeRoy Simms, one of the original fifteen, was charged but died a week before the trial. Someone shot him in the back through an open window. Plagued by nightmares and overcome with remorse, LeRoy had confessed his guilt before the grand jury and agreed to testify for the prosecution. He bled to death sitting in a rocking chair holding his baby. Old Mr. John Cooper was also charged but found unfit to stand trial. His brain was addled. The court remanded him to the care of his wife. Thomas Sanderson was already dead. Panicked by the fire, his horse slipped going down the bank toward the river and dragged Tom Boy into the water. The horse floundered but managed to cross. Tom Boy didn't drown, but his neck broke, and one leg twisted out of its socket. He died of pneumonia six weeks later.

Ben and Hugh Willard, once the last to arrive, were the first to go. Long before questions were asked and statements taken, before the grand jury met and charges filed, the Willard brothers saw the future. No guilt filled their mouths, no shame bowed their heads. Quietly, without obvious emotion, the Willard brothers pulled up stakes and were Gone to Texas.

Miss Toufet and I talked and visited the afternoon long. I think she liked me. I certainly liked her and hope she does well in her studies. Robert Toufet served in World War I and raised his family in Washington D.C. The last of his children, Miss Toufet's grandmother, had died this last year. Robert's brother James never married and rambled most of his life. He wound up in California working for the railroad.

Being young and hopeful, Miss Toufet wanted to know what happened to Alexander Toufet's property. Where were her great, great grandfather's things. The truth was there but not easy to tell. Everything not burned stood exactly where it was the night he died. It just belonged to whoever paid the taxes.

Before she left going back toward North Carolina, Grady rode her out to Mount Ebo Cemetery. The McDougles bury there. Most of the markers from that long ago don't have names, but Grady reckoned Alexander Toufet's place and took her picture by the grave. Then, she was on her way.

One thing did survive, one thing that could be hers: the brass handle of an old buggy whip. She seemed satisfied.

The Christmas Star

When Grandpa John died, the weather turned blistering hot and didn't let up all fall. Miss Busby's seventh grade room was the hottest place in the entire school and the house was an absolute oven. I couldn't get cool. Mama let me drag a mattress onto the back porch, but that was worse. The porch was twice as hot, and the floor made the mattress lumpy and hard. All I needed, which no one seemed to understand, was a little peace and quiet. People clucking around like chickens was worse than the heat. Then, Michael Wayne showed up. He appeared at the house Thanksgiving Day and had news of Rose.

Rose may be my sister, but she was never a nice person. We could say she ran away after she graduated from high school. But technically she didn't run away. Rose left. She took money that was not hers and just left. She didn't bother to say goodbye or when, if ever, she planned to come back. Rose was awful, but not Michael Wayne. Michael Wayne was handsome, smart, and lots of fun.

It was Thanksgiving afternoon and Grady and me had been out looking for a Christmas tree. We found a really tall, fat tree down in the George Field. After tying the ribbon around its trunk, we walked back to the house discussing how best to get the tree home. Grady thought we should go ahead and cut it off. We knew already it was too tall, but I favored carrying the entire tree back just in case.

Lots of people in town bought trees from the Lions Club. The Lions Club trees came from somewhere up in Minnesota. Even Jerry Jenkins whose dad ran the sale had to admit those trees were stupid. The big vacant lot where the Tiara Ballroom and Movie Theater used to be looked like an abandoned blue spruce forest and Mr. Jenkins the sad woodsman who lost Hansel and Gretel. Nobody should want those trees.

"The trees help poor people Cecil McRae," Jerry said. "The money buys stuff for crippled children, and eye glasses. Things like that."

"Well, somebody ought to go to Minnesota and find better trees," I suggested. "Those for sale are all dry and spiky. Your mother won't even buy one."

The Jenkinses had a fake tree. It was aluminum and came from Sears Roebuck in Meridian. It sat it in their picture window and changed colors at night.

Jerry's prissy sister Priscella Jane said. "We didn't want an old fashioned evergreen tree. We wanted an Evergleam tree. It's guaranteed to never shed needles and will stay shiny forever. Only rich people have them."

It had been one whole year, and we hadn't heard a word from Rose. Then there was Michael Wayne Duval sitting at the kitchen table talking and laughing. Mama liked him right away. He had loads of pictures. Every picture had some funny story he told about Rose and how popular she was. Rose and his wife Voncille were best friends. That's why he was at our house. Rose was on her way home and bringing Voncille.

It was amazing. Rose was coming home for Christmas and actually wanted to come.

Rose worked in Las Vegas. According to Michael Wayne, all Rose talked about was D'Leaux. How wonderful it was and how wonderful her life had been with us.

"If she's coming back," I asked, "why hasn't she called?"

"You must be Cecil McRae," Michael Wayne said. "I know all about you and how much Rose loves her baby sister. Rose wants everything to be a surprise, and she has a special surprise just for you. She told me so herself."

"What sort of surprise?"

"That won't do. That won't do at all," he said laughing like I didn't quite understand how things worked. "If I told you, it wouldn't be a surprise. Would it?"

That's how Michael Wayne Duval came to be at our house for Christmas. He knew how things worked and I didn't.

Rose was coming home and Mama didn't act the least bit mad. She was happy about the whole thing.

Voncille was moving to Florida because her mother had cancer. Michael Wayne didn't know exactly when they would get to D'Leaux. At least by Christmas Eve. Rose would be home for Christmas, then go on to Fort Lauderdale to help Voncille.

If you counted Mama's ladies' club, the Windham Masonic Lodge Order of the Eastern Star and everyone at Windham Presbyterian Church, half of Mounds County was coming by our house Christmas Eve. Mama called it a holiday open house.

She even asked the First Baptist youth choir to stop by for cocoa. They always caroled the nursing home and took fruit baskets to shut-ins. We were as busy as bees. Everything had to be extra special because of the open house and Rose.

During the day, Michael Wayne volunteered at the tree lot. Then in the evenings, he helped us decorate. He loved Christmas. It was his favorite time of year.

We got all new Christmas lights, the kind that blinked on and off. But before we started decorating, Michael Wayne and Grady spent one whole afternoon getting the tree to stand perfectly straight. It even brushed the ceiling just like I liked. By the time we finished, the limbs were so full of ornaments they should have sagged. Icicles, angel hair, and popcorn rope hung all around the sides even in the very back.

When we went looking for presents over in Moss, Michael Wayne bought a new star for the top. It was huge, gold, and had twinkly little lights around the edges. Mama didn't want him buying things for our tree but the star wasn't for us.

"It's for Rose, Mrs. Britton," he said, holding the star way up over his head "to guide her home. It's going to shine from D'Leaux, Mississippi, all the way through Louisiana across Texas and New Mexico straight to Las Vegas, Nevada."

"Besides," he added, "that tree deserves the most wonderful star we can find."

We had the most wonderful star and the prettiest tree ever. Even Mama agreed. From the tree, we moved on to the rest of the house. Garland, holly, candles, and dozens of crocheted snowflakes Grandma Rachel had made when she was a girl. By the time we finished, Christmas was in every room. We even wrapped the front door to make it a giant present complete with a red bow in the middle and jingle bells on the knob. In the living room as a final touch, we hung a big bunch of mistletoe I climbed up and got from an oak tree behind the barn. The days just flew by. I could hardly wait. We were having the best Christmas ever.

For the outside, we made cedar garland for the porch banister then frosted the front room windows with spray snow from Ben Franklin. Grady ran an extension cord from the pump house across the yard and wrapped lights around the mailbox. If it rained, the lights might short out, but Mama thought we could keep them lit at least until Rose got home.

When we weren't decorating, we were playing cards. Michael Wayne knew any card game you could name and could do magic tricks. One time he made the three of spades jump into Grady's pocket. Another time, the king of hearts ran away and hid somewhere on the Christmas tree. We nearly never found that card. It was in plain sight the whole time sticking out of the star. I laughed until I thought my sides would split. Grady got completely covered in angel hair trying to get it down. We finally left it were it was, and used a joker for the king. Once a long time ago, Michael Wayne had been a gambler headed down the wrong road. Voncille turned him around. He gave up gambling and started selling books.

According to Mr. Jenkins, Michael didn't actually sell books, he gave them away. Anyone buying a tree could pick a free book from the trunk of his car. Michael Wayne gave away so many books the Lions Club ran out of trees. Sold out for the first time ever.

"It's a marketing technique," Michael said. "Everyone loves to get something for free."

We played and played. My favorite was Crazy Eights. Rummy was Grady's game. Michael liked Battle and won every game. I didn't even mind losing. Losing to Michael Wayne felt better than winning. It was fun every time.

While we decorated and played cards, Mama cooked. Anyone coming to the open house needed something special just for them. First, she baked a white fruitcake like Rose liked. Then figgy pudding for her ladies' club. After that came gingerbread men and sugar cookies with colored icing for the choir. Michael Wayne liked divinity so she made a big batch of that and lots of fudge with marshmallow swirls for Grady and me.

"I am expecting you to serve the eggnog," Little Bit, Mama said. "Can you be extra careful not to spill on the tablecloth? And if Miss Sinclair comes, make sure Grady helps her mother get seated before you offer her refreshments."

Miss Sinclair was in Mama's ladies' club but didn't come to many meetings. When she wasn't teaching school, she had to mind her mother. Old Mrs. Sinclair didn't have any sense left and could only talk about her dead son Chester.

"Why does Old Mrs. Sinclair keep on about Chester, Mama?" I said. "She nearly drove me crazy last year at Homecoming. Chester this and Chester that. She never stops."

"A Japanese torpedo sank the ship he was on, Little Bit. No one survived."

"I know that," I said. "How could I forget? And Chester had his Uncle Roland's pocket watch and a book of verses he read from every night of his life. Mrs. Sinclair has only told the story fifty dozen times."

"Maybe you can be kind to Mrs. Sinclair, Cecil McRae, so kind that she forgets about Chester. Could you do that?" Mama asked. "Could you help Mrs. Sinclair forget to be sad?"

Christmas Eve night you couldn't hear yourself think. People laughing, hugging, wishing each other Merry Christmas, and kissing under my mistletoe. That was the best part. And I was really kind. I told Mrs. Sinclair about how Grady and me didn't buy a tree. We found our own down in the woods; we'd get them one too next year if they wanted. I made the story the longest I could and then got her some rum balls and sugar cookies. She liked those best.

Once the Baptists sang every Christmas song they knew, Jerry Jenkins ate three gingerbread men before taking a breath and then drank hot cocoa until it ran out. After it was gone, he had to want tea. Miss Hightower sang "O Holy Night" all by herself. Then in walked Uncle Dewey from Mobile carrying baby Robert Earl. I couldn't believe it. Uncle Dewey hardly ever came home since Aunt Ruby died, but there he was with a lady friend, Miss Dempsey, grinning like a Cheshire Cat. Nobody even thought of Rose..

Rose didn't come home for Christmas. She never came. Voncille's mother went ahead and died so they drove straight to Fort Lauderdale.

"I don't like Michael Wayne, Grady," I said. "I thought I did but I don't."

"Why not?" Grady asked.

"He left. He didn't say he was sorry or promise to come back or anything. He just left."

"He couldn't stay forever, Cecil McRae," Grady said. "He had to go to Florida. He doesn't live here."

"He ruined Christmas, Grady."

"He didn't ruin Christmas, Little Bit. If anybody ruined Christmas, it was Rose.

"I wish he'd never come, Grady. It's not fair for him to make everything so exciting and happy and then leave."

"I'm glad he came, Cecil McRae. Magic card tricks, those old books he gave away, the Christmas star. Even if he never comes back, I'm glad he came."

"Why glad, Grady."

"He helped us, Little Bit. He was so kind. For a little while, he helped us forget we were sad."

The Peanuts

Grandpa John loved Cuban cigars. They were his special luxury. He bought them by the box full from a mail order place in Baltimore. Dozens of yellow boxes littered with cigar bands and bits of stray tobacco nested under his bed, in his closet, and beside his old chair. It was my idea to clean out the house. Nothing had been done about the place since Mama died; and after years and years of sitting untouched, Grandpa's study was a good place to start.

That's when I first saw Lourdes LaFoche. At the dump. I had decided to throw away the cigar boxes. This woman was down in the gully digging through garbage, large, Hispanic, pregnant and cursing like a sailor. It had to be Lourdes LaFoche .Before I could speak, she reached into a heap of trash and pulled out an old moth eaten cap.

"Now you will see what I can do, Mr. Bigshot from America," she yelled waving that old piece of wool like a victory flag. "You and your precious family." With that said she spat on the trash heap, climbed the hill to her truck and drove off. She was like those women painted inside the lids of Grandpa John's cigar boxes.

Exotic, beautiful, and serene. Except Lourdes wasn't serene.

"Grady," I asked, "did you know Lourdes LaFoche speaks English?"

"Is that the new LaFoche wife, Little Bit? Brandon had his dog Poppa Pierre in the clinic last week but he didn't mention Lourdes."

"She was for sure talking about him down at the dump. I understood every word she said."

Lourdes LaFoche was Brandon LaFoche's second wife. He discovered her on a family trip after his first wife Sissy got killed. To help his pain, Brandon's brothers and cousins took him deep sea fishing in Guatemala. Brandon didn't bring home the typical trophy: a prize winning blue marlin, sailfish, or yellowfin tuna stuffed and mounted for his wall. He brought home Lourdes.

Poor Sissy. She left Brandon with four little girls and was actually pregnant with his boy when she died. It was a real tragedy. In the LaFoche family, men are expected to produce sons. A son announces true manhood and demands proper respect from the family. For that reason, a proper wife must produce baby after baby until the desired birth is achieved. A log truck making a bad turn onto the highway south of the old Beverly Brother's fruit stand drove a load of pine logs through Sissy's windshield. She and Betty Sue Dearmon didn't stand a chance. They had been over to Moss buying things for Sissy's layette. The two women were dead on the spot.

Sissy had barely cooled in the grave before Brandon installed Lourdes as her replacement.

The LaFoches are very successful business people. They're peanut farmers and maintain a tight knit community in the northwestern part of the county. LaFoches have lived there for generations, but they still claim to be Cajuns. People call them clannish and superstitious but no one calls them lazy. Every LaFoche male works in some way for the business and they marry according to family tradition. LaFoche girls are free to get grooms from anywhere they can. The girls marry out; they leave the family. LaFoche men get their brides from around Marksville in Avoyelles Parish, Louisiana. Those girls marry in. They come into the family and never leave. Lourdes LaFoche was the exception.

The first LaFoche in Mounds County must have left Louisiana sometime in the 1880's. That was Hebert LaFoche. Grandma Rachel remembered him from when her own Grandpa Teddy was alive. All the Mounds LaFoches come from him. He wore a red beret and sold parched peanuts on the streets of Windham. Today the peanut business is huge. LaFoche Family Farms owns or manages thousands of acres all producing peanuts. Their processing plant runs twenty-four hours a day seven days a week, but it's a closed operation. No one but LaFoche men work at the plant or on their farms. They speak French among themselves, and always, always have a Hebert LaFoche somewhere in the family.

They say "A Bear" instead of Hebert, and whichever one has the A Bear name is like a prince. He's the only one who doesn't work and he doesn't marry. He brings the luck. LaFoches believe without an A Bear in the family peanuts won't grow.

One of the A Bears was in Rose's class. Rose couldn't abide him. He was called Junior A Bear because an ancient old uncle was the real A Bear. Junior A Bear wouldn't kiss Rose.

"I'm an A Bear, Rose," he said. "Now leave me alone."

It was Rose's birthday. She was finally sweet sixteen and making the most of her day. Rose wanted to kiss sixteen boys. That was supposed to be lucky. No one objected except Junior A Bear. He didn't kiss girls.

"If I kiss a girl, I lose the luck, Rose," Junior explained. "Do you want me to lose the luck and make my family starve?"

"The kisses are for my luck, Junior," Rose pouted. "It's my birthday. Are you saying I can't be lucky because of some stupid peanuts?"

No matter what Rose did, however she threatened or teased, Junior A Bear wasn't interested.

She finally kissed Homer Langley. Homer was Mr. Masterson's pet and checked out books during fifth period. He volunteered to be kissed because of Junior. They were best friends. Rose was convinced bad luck would ruin her life if she missed one kiss. Homer wasn't her choice but he had to do.

Junior A Bear played the piano by ear and sounded like Jerry Lee Lewis. One time he sang "Mississippi Rag Mop" at an assembly and all the girls started screaming. When his car got hit by a train, the whole school went to the funeral.

"That was the most embarrassing funeral I have ever seen," Rose announced. "All those men crying. It's not like their mama died. And Junior, sitting on the railroad tracks like he didn't have good sense. How stupid was that?"

"I'm the lucky one, Cecil McRae, " she said. "Not some sissy boy too afraid to kiss a girl."

I thought about Junior A Bear after that day at the dump. I wondered if Lourdes' baby might be a boy; and if it was, would he be an A Bear.

"I loved my dog, Folks. Poppa Pierre was my best friend, my truest companion. This coon hunt with the Greys is to honor his memory."

"Brandon LaFoche, CEO of LaFoche Family Farms made those touching remarks at his news conference yesterday. They followed the announcement of a Letter of Intent between the LaFoche Family Farms and Greys Goodies, Inc. LaFoche will develop heart healthy strains of peanuts exclusively for Greys. The goal is to produce a peanut variety for organic dog foods. We at *The Monitor* applaud this act of love and loyal as we extend our continued condolences to Mr. LaFoche on the untimely death of his dog."

Mounds Monitor —Ed Winn reporting

"Grady," I asked, "What happened to Poppa Pierre? What did Ed Winn mean by untimely death?"

"He died of shock, Little Bit."

"Shock? Did that old dog get himself electrocuted?"

"It wasn't electricity, Cecil McRae. It was a knife. Poppa Pierre was mutilated. Someone cut off the dog's organs, wrapped them in an old beret, and threw them out at the processing plant. Brandon brought the dog in right away, but Poppa Pierre was too old to be castrated. The shock killed him."

I didn't throw away Grandpa's cigar boxes. I put them back in his room. It was the women. Those exotic beautiful serene women smiling from inside the lids. I couldn't throw them onto a garbage pile. I wondered what happened to those women, the real women. Were they tossed away somewhere to become human refuse? Or did they spit on the garbage heap, climb the hill to their truck, and drive off.

The Grave

Here he lies where he long'd to be;
Home is the sailor, home from the sea,
And the hunter home from the hill.
—*Robert Louis Stevenson*

Tommy Gaines was the first principal of the new D'Leaux Elementary School. After Buell McPherson died, he resigned and went to live in Tucson, Arizona. He didn't want to go and said so to anyone who would listen. But he did go. In assembly that last day he cried in front of the whole school.

Maybe he did have asthma. That's what he said. Tucson may have been an easier place to breathe. But Mr. Tommy didn't leave because of unhealthy air. He left because of three old maids: Elva Mae, Connie and Jewel McPherson. Elva Mae, Connie and Jewel despised Thomas Gaines and ran him out of town.

Then they got upset with Old Mrs. Sinclair over a tombstone. Mrs. Sinclair thought the Navy had found her son Chester and buried him at Windham. She grieved for years. Chester didn't come home from the war. The Japanese sank his ship and he was lost. Over the years, Mrs. Sinclair became confused. When she started putting flowers on Tommy Gaines' headstone, Elva Mae, Connie and Jewel became so upset they left the Windham Presbyterian Church and became Baptists.

Buell McPherson, their brother, was Superintendent of Mounds County Schools. Buell died in a car wreck on his way to Moss. Before that he was a Marine and a hero. He liberated the Philippines then helped out in Korea. He could have been a general but decided not to.

"All Douglas MacArthur does is shake hands and sign papers," Elva Mae said. "Our brother has better things to do."

I don't remember Buell coming home; he seemed to be there all of my life until he died. But sometime after he decided not to become a general, Buell came back to Mounds County and built a house on the McPherson place next to his sisters. That's when Thomas Gaines first came to Mounds. He helped with Buell's house. They had island hopped with MacArthur and were best friends.

"It was a wet tent and monsoon rains for three years," Mr. Tommy said. "We're ready for better quarters."

Mr. Tommy built the house while Buell ran the schools.

Everything about the house was new. It must have been the first totally new house I had ever seen. New and fancy. The windows had drapes not curtains and all the furniture matched on purpose. Hanging lanterns, Geisha girl clothes, and pretty paper umbrellas decorated every room.

"It's all Tommy's doing," Buell said laughing. "Tommy Gaines loves tea houses so we have to live in one."

We're kin to the McPhersons but not exactly. Idabelle Horn, Grandma Rachel's cousin, married Buell's father, George

McPherson. She was an old maid and had come from Meridian to be the teacher at Box Corner School. They married after his first wife died. Cousin Idabelle became mother to Mr. George's children even though she was too old to have any of her own.

I never knew Cousin Idabelle and Mr. George. They were gone long before I was born and are buried in the church cemetery. Cousin Idabelle rests on one side of Mr. George and his first wife Cynthia Taylor on the other. Buell's there too beside his mother. McPhersons now lie up and down all over their plot, but for years Mr. George, his two wives, and Buell were pretty much left alone.

Mr. Tommy taught fourth grade then got to be principal once the new elementary school was ready and we could move in. Everybody liked Mr. Tommy. He was kind and funny, and loved to read stories. *A Christmas Carol* was my favorite. He could sound just like Uncle Scrooge and made the Tiny Tim part really sad.

Elva Mae, Connie and Jewel didn't care that we liked Mr. Tommy or that he was Buell's best friend. Once Buell was gone, they kicked him out.

"If Buell had wanted that man to have something, he would have it now. He has no right to claim things after the fact," Elva Mae said. "Certainly not Buell's house. It's best he be gone and be gone today."

Mr. Tommy didn't go to the funeral. He just stopped being principal and left. He never called anyone or said he was coming back. But he did plan to come back. It was only a question of time. Sanderson Monument Company installed a matching tombstone next to Buell in the McPherson plot. They put Mr. Tommy's name and birthday across the top and wrote a poem across the bottom.

Elva Mae, Connie and Jewel were outraged, but Mrs. Sinclair thought the handsome blue granite headstone was Chester's. His favorite poem was on it. The book of verses he read each night and his Uncle Roland's watch were still lost, but Chester was found.

"That headstone has nothing to do with Chester Sinclair," Elva Mae insisted. "And the Navy didn't put it there! That man, that awful evil man, has put his marker where he doesn't belong. We want it moved."

It made no difference what Elva Mae, Connie or Jewel might want, where the headstone sat, or even whose name was on it. Mrs. Sinclair knew the truth. The grave belonged to Chester. Chester was found. He was home at last.

"I waited," Mrs. Sinclair said, putting her flowers on the grave for Homecoming the next day. "I waited because I knew my boy would come home. So many were lost, but mine came home."

"Thomas Robert Gaines, former resident of Mounds County, will be buried Thursday, July 23, at Windham Presbyterian Church. The Reverend James Monroe will officiate at the graveside service. Mr. Gaines served in the Pacific during World War II and was an educator. Friends may make memorial contributions to the D'Leaux Elementary School Library or Boys and Girls Clubs of America."

Mounds Monitor —Ed Winn reporting

A small crowd assembled under the green tent from McElroy Funeral Home. Brother Monroe conducted a brief service with efficient dignity and unaffected regard; and the earth accepted the body to rest in Christian repose.

Tommy Gaines claimed his place. He was home at last.

The Homecoming

Homecoming at Windham Presbyterian Church was last Sunday. Such a wonderful day. Unlike any I may see again. I lost my purse. The purse Grady's wife Evelyn gave me as a birthday present. The purse she decided I had to carry and that I had tried to like.

The crisis with the purse was on account of Maude Standard dying. She owned Maude's Standard Florist in D'Leaux and had handled my flower needs for years.

With Maude gone, I had given Brother Elisha Williams the job. Brother Williams runs a florist shop/tuxedo rental business in the Magnolia Mart Shopping Center. He's right next door to Dottie Ingram's In-Style Salon. Brother Williams preaches at Ram-in-the-Bush-on-Holy-Mount Baptist Church and sings baritone in a Black gospel quartet. Coming and going from my appointments with Dottie, I often speak with Brother Williams. We had discussed what I needed in flowers some weeks back and he was keeping the store open until six Saturday afternoon for the pick up.

My cards, my checks, everything I needed was in that purse. With Maude, my credit was established but not with Brother

Williams. He would let me have the flowers, I knew that. But expecting special treatment might put him in an awkward position. It was my first order and a large one for a small shop. Grady would help but I hesitated to call.

" Grady is not to be disturbed on Saturday." Evelyn had decided.

"Grady is staying home on Saturdays. Unless I said otherwise, he would be gone by sunrise doing God knows what. Your brother is a scatter brain, Cecil McRae. Unless it is an absolute emergency he is to be left alone with his wife."

It was an absolute emergency, so I called.

"You're not bothering anybody, Little Bit," Grady said. "I'm glad to help. Let's get those flowers."

We drove to Brother Williams' and Grady paid the bill. I was relieved. Brother Williams did a beautiful job. The seven arrangements were in the cooler ready to go. Each one tucked inside a clear plastic cleaner's bag sealed with a white corsage pin.

Once we got to the church, Grady insisted I sit on the bench behind Mama's grave. He would place the flowers if I would direct.

"Those red roses are for Mama," I said. "The yellow glads for Grandma Rachel. Grandpa John gets the sunflowers, Grady. You know how he loved that patch of sunflowers Trudy Evans planted every year."

With great care Grady removed the pins, extracted the arrangements, and with awkward tenderness adjusted the flowers for their best effect. Daddy gets something blue. Mama always said she loved him first for his blue eyes. Every year, I honor that love and those blue eyes. Great Grandmother Elizabeth gets white roses even though they don't last long and Great Grandpa Willard, Lily of the Valley. Augustus Horn gets red poppies. He was Great Grandma Dickens' brother and the hope of her family. But he died at seventeen.

By the time we finished, twilight was gathering and a small breeze beginning to stir. One can't put flowers out too early or the sun ruins them before Sunday. If one waits too late, darkness catches hold not to mention the mosquitoes.

Grady had never helped with the flowers. Mama did them until she died. Since she was gone, I hadn't asked. When he married Evelyn, Grady left Windham Presbyterian and joined First Baptist in town. Evelyn decided they would be more comfortable in a larger church. To leave Windham was one of the many decisions Evelyn made. She decided something every day.

"A man doesn't know what he wants," she would say. "It's up to his wife to decide. Where to go. What to do. Even what to think. Grady would be completely lost without me. As his wife, I know what's best; I just do. And as my husband, he agrees. That's the foundation of a successful marriage, Cecil McRae. If you ever marry, you'll understand these things."

I never spoke with Grady about his leaving and have tried not to resent Evelyn for taking him away. They only attend Windham for Homecoming and the occasional funeral.

Homecoming itself begins at eleven o'clock the first Sunday in August. The Reverend James T. Monroe is serving as interim pastor. Brother Monroe, presently retired, served Windham twenty-five years ago. He's back holding things together until a new pastor can be found. The Reverend Hollis Mercier was guest speaker for the day. Brother Hollis grew up in Windham and the church helped put him through seminary. It was a joy seeing them together again.

Brother Hollis preached on food and the different foods we eat in various environments of life. I don't remember the Biblical text but the metaphor was effective. His final point was about food at home.

"Food at home is unique," Brother Hollis said. "It alone is prepared especially for us and most importantly it is prepared with love. Remember Dear Friends, home for us, for us Christians, is the church. Jesus is calling, calling you home to your family. Come home," he concluded. "Come home today and take your place at the table."

When she was sure the sermon had ended, Marjorie McIlwain launched into the last hymn "O, Zion's Haste." Marjorie had to step down as pianist due to a weak heart, but still plays for Homecoming each year. Singing to her accompaniment is like breathing fresh air on a cool spring day.

During the last chorus, Reverend Monroe made his way toward the back. Thin and tottery, he looks more like a daddy long legs wearing a suit than a man. Steadying himself by the door he raised an arm to pronounce the benediction. Just at that moment, Grady slipped out of the pew and stood by his side.

Reverend Monroe said the benediction, then embraced Grady. "Welcome home, Grady," he said. "Welcome home at last."

For an instant, the building held its breath. Not a sound, not a flutter. I didn't look at Evelyn, but I felt the shock. Everyone did. She was Pharaoh's army a single second before the Red Sea assault: utterly surprised.

For the first time in her ten-year marriage, Evelyn did not decide.

The tables in the pavilion fairly groaned under the abundance of food. Ice melted before it could cool the tea, and people laughed and hugged.

Compliments on her sweet potato surprise sustained Evelyn through the long afternoon. That and the strength of her new silk suit. The big square buttons of the magenta jacket struggled mightily holding things together.

The day ended with many tearful good-bye kisses and promises to come again.

Just before dark, I parked the car by the side of the house and walked onto the back porch. Right inside the door in plain sight lay my missing purse. That big black deflated squash of a bag looked ashamed of itself, embarrassed for being there. Honestly, I don't think that purse liked me and was trying to leave. Constructed of bullet-proof-vest material complete with steel zippers and padded straps, it needed to ride the shoulders of a female superhero not Evelyn Britton's old maid sister-in-law. Everything has a proper place, a home. That purse knew its home was not with me. I agreed and let it go.

Homecoming is over. The flowers faded. The dishes washed. Everything is home, home at last in its proper place. And I have a new purse. That purse and I get along just fine. Mary Leigh Strengthford made it. Mary Leigh sews for a living. She has three small children to raise with only a sewing machine for help. I buy her purses crooked seams and all. It's the kind thing to do.

Discussion Guide
for
D'Leaux, Mississippi

LIFE BETWEEN MOSS AND TUCKERTOWN

These stories chronicle events that mark Cecil McRae as she grows from childhood into womanhood. The stories are full of "ah ha" moments. Spend a few minutes recalling "ah ha" moments in your own life.

Share those experiences with the group and explain how the event changed you or brought you a new understanding.

One element often running through the stories is the unknown, the unexplained. The word "magic" comes up often in the stories. The characters seem to accept this element in their lives just as they accept the past. Identify some examples of the unexplained.

THE RABBIT TRAP: PAGE 1

Adults do not seem to hold Alice Faye accountable for her outrageous behavior. Why? Cecil McRae's things were returned. Who may have returned them? What does the return tell us?

THE BOBWHITES: PAGE 7

Boxes populate this story. What purposes do the various boxes serve? Cecil McRae cries when the bobwhites are released. What are the reasons for her tears?

THE AMI DU COEUR: PAGE 13

Why do the people of D'Leaux tolerate Miss Estelle? Are the things Miss Estelle tells Rose and the other girls true? What does having a pet goat say about Miss Estelle?

THE CURSE: PAGE 19

Baxter Sandstrom Willard cursed his family. How did the will affect his sons? What did he leave his wife? Consider how that request might ultimately be a blessing. Why was his daughter spared?

THE SILVER DOLLARS: PAGE 23

The term "savage" is used to describe the natives that chased Miss Everhart and also Cecil McRae, Grady, and Jerry. In each case, is the description appropriate? Why or why not? Who was embarrassed? Why?

THE CHRISTMAS GIFT: PAGE 29

Grady and Cecil McRae find a Gypsy baby. Their mother did not allow them to take gifts from the thankful Gypsies. Why? What was the Christmas gift and who received it? Was more than one gift given and received? Explain.

THE HONEYMOON: PAGE 37

The humor in The Honeymoon springs from a misunderstanding of the word. What was the misunderstanding? Where would Cecile McRae go on a honeymoon? Why was the choice problematic? What was Jerry's attitude toward Miss Edna's honeymoon? Where would Jerry go?

WASHINGTON D.C.: PAGE 43

How did John McRae prove his love to Rachel Willard? What could he have offered her? What effect does the love story have on Cecil McRae?

THE PIANO RECITAL: PAGE 51

What did Cecil McRae realize about Mr. Thompson and Miss Edna that indicates her maturing view of the world?

THE UNDERWEAR: : PAGE 55

The Underwear explores the idea of secrets. What are the secrets? What secret does Cecil McRae realize about Rose that would keep Rose from ever coming home?

THE CATS: PAGE 65
Why were the girls sleeping on Cecil McRae's porch?

THE KIDNAPPING: PAGE 73
The term "kidnapping" is used to explain the two disappearances of Edwina Murray. She was taken for different reasons. What were they? How does the kidnapping affect Edwina?

THE DOUGHNUTS: PAGE 79
What motivated Grandma Rachel to give Cecil McRae the packet of letters and pictures? What was she trying to tell Mr. Mangum about Cousin Irene? Why did Cecil McRae react so violently to Miss Beasley? What was her dilemma concerning what she learned?

THE PLAY: PAGE 87
The Play explores how the two sexes manipulate each other. Who manipulates whom? Is the manipulation successful? How?

THE TOP HAT CLUB: PAGE 93
Theft and deception propel The Top Hat Club. What things were stolen? Who practices deception and on whom? Cecil McRae is angry and confused. Why? What is Grady's observation about people? Do you agree?

THE CHICKEN SALAD: PAGE 99
The Chicken Salad explores service to others. How are Wanda and Evelyn both alike and different? Why does Cecil McRae prefer Wanda to The Auxiliary?

THE GRIEF PROCESS: PAGE 105

Why is Tyler so upset with Lloyd Dunn? What reason does Grady give to explain Tyler's reaction to Maude's burial? What does his explanation say about Tyler? Why does Cecil McRae feel connected to Oprah? Can Lloyd find love again? For Lloyd, where might that love be found?

THE ORANGE POPPIES: PAGE 111

What awareness does Cecil McRae discover in herself that her mother and grandmother seem not to have?

THE FEED STORE: PAGE 113

What details in the yard, around the barn, and with Randal, announce something is out of joint. What does Randal show Cecile McRae? How does Cecil McRae deal with what she saw? How does the reader know Chambliss Willard was complicit in the tragedy?

THE BEAUTY PAGEANT: PAGE 117

The Pre-Teen Queen contest is a huge success in D'Leaux. How are Dee Dee and her sister Sandra the real winners? What is the truth about being the queen of D'Leaux? Why doesn't J. J. Cooper's behavior upset Cecil McRae and Grady?

MISS TOUFET: PAGE 123

Cecil McRae reaches back in family history to tell Miss Toufet the story of Alexander Toufet. Why would Cecil McRae know that story so well? What is the difference in the burials of Julian Horn and Alexander Toufet? Miss Toufet is a descendant of Alexander Toufet. How many generations of Toufets have lived that trauma?

THE CHRISTMAS STAR: PAGE 131
What reason does Michael give for coming to D'Leaux? What seems to be the true reason for his visit? What did Cecil McRae do during the party that mirrors Michael's behavior?

THE PEANUTS: PAGE 139
"Marrying out" or "marrying in" defines the function of women in the LaFoche family? What is that function? What makes Lourdes different? How does she announce her defiance? Could Junior LaFoche's death have also been an act of defiance? Why couldn't Junior just run away?

THE GRAVE: PAGE 145
Grief can overrun reason. How does it overrun Mrs. Sinclair? Anger has overrun Buell's sisters. Why do the sisters hate Mr. Tommy and run him out of town? Should the marker be moved? Why or why not.

THE HOMECOMING: PAGE 149
Purses define Evelyn and Cecil McRae. What do the purses say about each woman? Why can Cecil McRae be satisfied and Evelyn not? Why is Grady's return to Windham Presbyterian Church a change in his relationship with Evelyn?

Notes

Notes

Acknowledgements

A special thanks to the writers of the Ocean Springs Writing Group: Melissa Johnson, Barbara Jones, Sheila Turner, Susan Skaggs, Alex Blevens, and the late Russell Thompson. I must further thank Melissa and her dear mother Sally Johnson for their careful copy edit. Also, Linda Schroeder, Nancy Wilson, Darlene Stuart, Gail Bishop, Princie Graham, and Karlyn Stephens, your kindness is my continued treasure. Thank you.

About the Author

Cecil George Brown lives with her husband on the Mississippi Gulf Coast. She also maintains a residence in Wayne County where Scottish ancestors settled before statehood. Those determined pioneers, for good or for bad, are not forgotten.